Murder at a Yard Sale

A Myrtle Clover Cozy Mystery, Volume 22

Elizabeth Spann Craig

Published by Elizabeth Spann Craig, 2023.

MURDER AT A YARD SALE

First edition. May 18, 2023.

Written by Elizabeth Spann Craig.

In memory of Daddy and Amma

Chapter One

"The hole is too deep, Dusty. Fill it in a little."

Dusty, Myrtle's ancient yardman, leaned on his shovel and glared at her. "You done told me to make the hole deeper."

"Yes, but not *that* deep, Dusty. Pay attention! The poor tree will perish if you bury it. Its root collar will be under dirt."

Dusty appeared to be gritting his teeth as he tossed a shovelful of red clay back into the hole he was digging.

Myrtle's friend Miles, who was sitting beside Myrtle, winced in sympathy. "You might be wearing Dusty out," he murmured.

"Dusty might be wearing *me* out," retorted Myrtle. "Every time he puts the tree into the hole, it's either practically underground or it's perched on a mound of dirt. There must be a halfway point."

"I kin hear you, you know," muttered Dusty. "Nuthin' wrong with my ears." He narrowed his eyes at Myrtle. "Anyway, the most important thing is to *water* the tree. This ain't the right time of year to be planting 'em."

"I had no control over that, as I mentioned. I won the raffle for garden club and was presented with this wispy dogwood. I'm going to put all of my considerable energies into ensuring the tree does well. I'm very motivated. Besides, it's a perfectly acceptable time of year to plant. I looked it up online."

"Fall is better," said Dusty. "Plus, this is the same spot you had another tree. An' that one died." He put the tree back in and looked questioningly at Myrtle.

"Now the tree is sitting up too high. Take just a smidge of soil back out again."

Miles looked uneasily at Dusty's stormy expression. He said, "Let's go inside for a spell, Myrtle."

"But we're having a picnic." Myrtle indicated their plates which held pimento cheese sandwiches and boiled peanuts they'd gotten from Crazy Dan, a somewhat unstable individual who was their friend's brother.

"We can bring the food inside."

Myrtle stood up and then looked at Dusty who was now covered with red clay. "I do have some food for you, Dusty. Pimento cheese."

Dusty spat into the soil. "Too exotic for me."

Myrtle stared at him. "I didn't have you pegged as a picky eater. Puddin isn't creative enough to handle a picky eater."

Dusty was now glaring at her again. "I make my own meals."

"That can't be true. I've heard Puddin raving over the chicken pot pies she makes."

Dusty grunted. "Sometimes I eat what she makes. Sometimes I eat my own food, and she eats her own food."

"Hm. Well, to each his own. So no pimento cheese for you."

"Nope," said Dusty. "I will take some of them boiled peanuts, though."

"Done. I'll set them out on the kitchen counter in a bowl."

Dusty started shaking his head. "Gotta eat 'em outside. If I track red clay into yer kitchen, Puddin'll have my hide."

Puddin was Myrtle's lackadaisical housekeeper. "Considering it would be tough for me to even persuade Puddin to come over on the *premise* of cleaning, I have to agree with you. I'd end up having to scrub the floor myself and at my age, the floor and I aren't particularly well-acquainted."

So Myrtle put together a large bowl of boiled peanuts, and Miles stuck them outside on the bench where he and Myrtle had been sitting.

"Are we eating in the kitchen?" asked Miles.

"Let's bring the food into the living room. We can watch our soap opera."

"I do wish you'd stop saying that."

"Why? It *is* our soap opera. Stop pretending you don't enjoy *Tomorrow's Promise* as much as I do."

It was true. Miles had, against all odds, gotten hooked on a show that included tropes like alien abductions, returns from the dead, and amnesia.

"Perhaps it's true," admitted Miles. "But it should stay our secret."

Myrtle liked having secrets. "I'll work on that."

She turned on their show, which she'd taped earlier. They tried to stay one day behind on *Tomorrow's Promise* so that they could watch it whenever it suited them. When the show opened, there seemed to be a lot going on. Adelaide and Benjamin were having a terrible argument about going to the South of France. The argument was taking place in the hospital where Benjamin had just had brain surgery.

"This seems especially dramatic," said Miles. "Surely Adelaide can see their vacation can't possibly proceed. Benjamin might not even make it out of the hospital."

Myrtle paused the show so they could discuss the issue. "But remember that Adelaide believes Benjamin is conjuring excuses to avoid spending time with her because he's having an affair."

Miles raised his eyebrows. "Brain surgery as an excuse?"

"Well, perhaps Adelaide is a bit warped. But Benjamin isn't helping matters."

She hit play again and the show continued. As was the norm with the soap opera, the scene ended with Adelaide and Benjamin staring meaningfully at each other. Another scene started, this one involving a woman who'd been kidnapped and was being held for ransom by a masked bandit.

There was a sudden, loud knock on the door. Myrtle and Miles both jumped violently.

"Mercy!" said Myrtle. "Who on earth is that?"

She got up to find out, and Miles quickly took the remote and turned off the television so the evidence of his interest in soap operas wouldn't be on display.

"Red!" bellowed Myrtle when she opened the door to see her son standing there. "What on earth are you doing? You nearly scared the spit out of me."

Red glowered at her. "You nearly scared the spit out of *me*. You didn't answer your phone. I called you. A lot."

"Did you? Well, I clearly didn't hear it. You might have called when Miles and I were sitting in the backyard with Dusty."

"What about your landline phone? I tried calling that one, too," said Red. He finally noticed Miles was there and bobbed his head politely at him. "Hi there, Miles."

"Hi Red."

Myrtle put her hands on her hips. "I had the landline disconnected. All I was getting was spam calls. At first the calls were almost entertaining. I'd act as if I were someone who could easily be duped and I could tell the unscrupulous person on the other end was getting very excited. Then I'd hang up on them."

"Sounds like loads of fun." Red rolled his eyes.

"It was. But then the number of calls grew, and it became completely untenable. Day and night. So I had the phone disconnected." Myrtle shrugged coolly.

"I don't like it," said Red. He had his own hands on his hips now. "I want you to reach a phone easily in case you need to."

"Fortunately, I just happen to have a phone I can fit into my pocket. Who needs a landline?"

Red said, "But you *don't* put it in your pocket. It's inside when you're outside. Or it's at home when you're at the store. It's a problem." He turned to Miles. "Do *you* have your phone on you right now?"

Miles gave Myrtle an apologetic look before pulling his own phone out of the pocket of his khaki pants.

Myrtle narrowed her eyes at him. "Traitor," she murmured. Then she said blithely, "Well, clearly, all is well that ends well. I wasn't in any danger. I was watching Dusty butcher the planting of the tree I won at garden club. Then Miles and I were inside watching our soap opera."

Miles winced. Clearly, Myrtle was getting him back.

Red seemed to be hiding a smile at the mention of their show.

"Anyway," said Myrtle, "I could just open a window and holler if I needed you. You're right across the street."

"What if you fell and couldn't reach the phone? Your hips are over eighty years old. They might not take well to falling."

Myrtle scowled at him. "What if you leave my hips out of this? I don't like it when you talk as if parts of me were some sort of disembodied things. Besides, have you forgotten about *this*?" She waved her medic alert necklace at him. "Or have you just forgotten it's not mere jewelry?"

Red now seemed more subdued. "Actually, I did forget about it. But I still think you should have your phone on you. In one of your pockets, just like Miles does."

"I don't *have* any pockets in these pants. I blame this on male fashion designers. I'd rather have the pockets, but the designers disagree."

Red now looked eager to leave, since his point had been made. "Fine. All right, I'll leave you alone. And I'll go see if I can find more pants for you that have pockets."

"Good."

"Maybe some cargo pants." Red's lips quirked at the thought.

Myrtle glared at him as he walked out the door. "He's so very annoying."

Miles said, "On the upside, he cares about you. He wants to make sure you're all right."

"He's just more focused on his responsibility than he is on me. He doesn't like falling down on the job. Anyway, it's the final straw. Before Dusty leaves, I'll have him pull my gnomes out. Particularly that giant one that Red despises so much."

Miles was unsurprised at the mention of gnomes. He handed her the remote. "What makes it the final straw?"

"Red wants to come along on my doctor visits now. As if I were a child! Can you imagine?"

Miles said mildly, "I've always read that it's good to have a patient advocate with you during appointments."

"He's not advocating during the visits, though. He's being an alarmist. He brings up everything that could possibly be wrong with me—stuff he's looked up on the internet. He questions my doctor as if he were a suspect in a murder investigation. My memory, my heart, my lungs—he inquires about everything. He looked up that rash I had on my arm online and was convinced it was some sort of dreadful pox. It's all very irritating."

Dusty stuck his head through the kitchen door. "I'm leavin'."

"Not yet! I need you to pull out the gnomes."

Dusty balked. "That weren't what you told me when you called me."

"Yes, I know. But Red has committed more transgressions. The gnomes are entirely necessary."

Dusty muttered something under his breath that Myrtle was glad she couldn't hear.

"You don't have to take all of them out. But I definitely want that big guy to be front and center. Directly in front of Red's house."

"Poor Elaine," murmured Miles. He often felt sorry for Red's wife when Myrtle had the gnomes pulled out.

"Elaine likes the big gnome," said Myrtle. "That's because Jack loves it. My grandson, of course, is remarkable. Elaine says Jack looks out his window and sings a goodnight song to the giant gnome before he goes to sleep."

Dusty seemed unimpressed by the story. "I got stuff to do."

"Set a timer on your phone. Spend fifteen minutes pulling out gnomes and then stop."

Dusty gave her a doubtful look. "An' that'll be enough?"

"Absolutely."

There was more muttering of a dire nature from Dusty, but he seemed to acquiesce.

"Now let's get back to our show," said Myrtle. "And I certainly hope there are no further interruptions."

But five more minutes into an intriguing and rather confusing scene involving a character who'd been cloned, Myrtle's phone rang.

"For heaven's sake," hissed Myrtle. She hit the pause button again. "At this rate, we'll never figure out what's going on with this show."

"I'm not sure if I could figure it out even without interruptions," said Miles. "And at least you found your phone."

It was true. The formerly AWOL phone was lodged under the chair cushion.

"Hello?" inquired Myrtle impatiently.

"Myrtle. It's Georgia."

Georgia was not usually one of the people who interrupted Myrtle's day. That honor ordinarily went to Red or Tippy Chambers. Myrtle's interest was piqued.

"Georgia? Is everything okay?"

Miles lifted his eyebrows in surprise. He also knew Georgia didn't often call on Myrtle. Additionally, he was rather fascinated by Georgia. With all her tattoos and her loud and gruff demeanor, she reminded him of someone he'd been in the service with.

Georgia said, "Sure, everything is okay. You know me! I can handle just about everything you throw at me."

This was true. Georgia was, overall, a very matter-of-fact person.

"But you're probably wondering why I'm calling. I'm having a yard sale tomorrow. I mean, I should have had the thing when I decided to move six months ago, but I couldn't be bothered. I guess there's no time like the present. Anyway, I wanted to publicize it a little. I wondered if you were still doing the newspaper's social media stuff."

Myrtle was a columnist for the *Bradley Bugle*. But she also fondly considered herself a crime reporter. Bradley had become something of a hotbed for crime. She was beginning to think something might be in the water.

"Actually, Elaine has been doing the social media for the paper for a little while. You know she has that interest in photography."

"Mm." Georgia's tone was noncommittal.

Myrtle understood. Although Elaine was always very enthusiastic about her hobbies and devoted to learning the craft behind them, they rarely ended up well. Her photography for the newspaper often included bits of Elaine's thumb.

Myrtle said, "But she's really good at putting up a little graphic design."

"Got it. I figured that might be the best way to advertise it, you know? Is it free to have it listed on the newspaper's social media?"

"Sure it is. But it's already the middle of the day. If you want to make sure people see it, you should go ahead to call Elaine and let her know. It should be a good time for her—Jack takes his nap around now," said Myrtle.

"Will do. Do you think you might come around? I'm going to have all kinds of great stuff out there. You need to come and shop."

The only problem with that was that Georgia and Myrtle didn't exactly share the same tastes. Myrtle reflected on the time she'd gone to Georgia's house to see that she'd repurposed a coffin as a coffee table. And Georgia was very fond of her angel collection. Myrtle's tastes ran more to obnoxious gnomes. Although, she remembered, Georgia had actually been the one who'd found the giant gnome in the first place.

"What kinds of things are you selling?" asked Myrtle cautiously.

"Oh, all kinds of stuff! Tell Miles to come, too. I know he's probably sitting there with you now."

Miles blushed as if Georgia could see him through the phone.

"I'll have a drumkit there. And some furniture. I gotta make more room for my angel collection."

"At the expense of your furniture?" asked Myrtle.

"Why not? I live by myself, so it's not like I need a million places to sit. And the angels make me feel . . . serene."

It was an interesting choice of words for the gruff Georgia.

"But I *am* going to sell a few of my angels. I gotta make space for more of them. So a few of my least-favorites will go up for sale. Maybe you'd even like one. I could visit my angels at your house, if you decided to buy one."

"We'll be there," promised Myrtle.

"Miles, too?"

"I'll be sure to bring him along."

Myrtle hung up, and Miles looked a little uncomfortable. "What's wrong now?" asked Myrtle.

"I always feel a certain level of discomfort attending yard sales. Don't you?"

Myrtle crinkled her brow. "No. Should I?"

"It's hard, isn't it? You're walking around, passing judgment on everyone's most prized possessions."

Myrtle shook her head. "No. If they were their most prized possessions, they wouldn't be on sale in their front yard."

"Regardless, it's tough. I'll feel pressure to get *something*. Otherwise, it's almost as if I was only there to gawk at Georgia's personal things and pass judgment on them. It feels prurient."

Myrtle said, "Don't be so sensitive, Miles. Heavens. We're simply going to pop by and say hi to Georgia. I haven't even been in her new house since she moved. I'll glance around at her merchandise. We'll resist the urge to purchase anything. We'll ask how it's going. Then we'll have breakfast at the diner."

Miles sighed. "And when are we making this expedition?"

"Early. You know how it is with yard sales. All the good stuff is gone by eight o'clock."

"You just said we weren't going to buy anything!" said Miles.

"And we won't. But that doesn't mean I don't want to see what she has available. After all, she uses a coffin for a coffee table." Myrtle picked up the remote. "Now where were we?"

"Samantha was cloned," said Miles glumly.

"Strange storyline. Okay."

They continued watching the show, which veered between the various storylines so quickly that their heads fairly spun. There was one other interruption when Dusty stuck his head back in the door to collect money from Myrtle for the yard work and gnome work. But aside from that, they could finish the latest episode.

Miles stretched. "I think I should head back home now. I've got to mull over that episode."

"Yes, me too. I might have nightmares about the alien abduction tonight. Poor Shawna. See you later, Miles."

Myrtle had just finished tidying up the boiled peanut bowl and their plates and cups when there was another tap at her front door.

Chapter Two

"Mercy," muttered Myrtle. She'd been planning to start work on her crossword and wondered if her puzzle time was going to be as incessantly interrupted as her soap opera time had been.

It was Miles. He looked a little confused.

Myrtle stepped aside to let him in. "Did you forget your phone again?"

He shook his head. He was holding a letter. "I just checked my mail and got something."

Myrtle waved him to the sofa. "A real letter? Usually, you and I only get junk mail and bills."

"A letter from my daughter," Miles said slowly as he absently sat on the sofa.

"Really? She sends letters? I thought the younger folks didn't even know how to do that anymore. I'm not even sure *I* know how to do that anymore."

Miles smiled. "Well, she's a bit of an old soul. Anyway, she and her kids are coming to visit."

This was also unusual. Myrtle hadn't known them to visit before. Miles had made the visit out there once or twice. But it definitely wasn't an everyday thing. "When are they coming?"

"Tomorrow, I think."

"*Tomorrow?*"

Miles said, "The letter must have taken a long while to get here."

"Well, they live on the other side of the country, don't they? Mercy. She's lucky you didn't have any plans." Myrtle paused. "I'm meeting them, of course."

"Of course you are."

Myrtle thought some more about this. "I should perhaps host them here."

"I don't think that's necessary," demurred Miles. "Thank you."

"Your place is too small for a daughter and two teenagers."

Miles nodded. "They're planning on staying at that hotel that's by the lake."

"Mm. Okay. Then you'll need activities. Events to entertain them while they're here. I could host a dinner party."

Miles hastily said, "No. I don't want you going to the trouble."

"It's no trouble at *all*, Miles. It's what friends do for each other when they have family coming from Washington state."

"California, actually. But I think we should just play everything by ear. A dinner party might make them feel awkward. You know."

Myrtle didn't know. But she wanted to be agreeable since this was such an unusual occurrence. "Maybe we'll go out to eat, then."

Now Miles looked a bit gloomy. "There really aren't any nice restaurants in town."

"What? The diner is perfectly nice. What's more, it has *character*."

Miles said, "The diner has signs on the walls advising its patrons to avoid profanity."

"An excellent tactic. Anyway, it serves as local color," said Myrtle with a shrug. "Besides, your family is here to see you and all your haunts. That way, they can picture what you're doing here in Bradley. Did they come visit you when you lived in Atlanta?"

"They did. But it's easier to get to Atlanta, obviously. They have a major airport. Now they'll have to fly into Charlotte and drive over. It's going to be more of a trip."

Myrtle said, "One they're clearly happy to make."

Miles looked rather conflicted, which bothered Myrtle. To keep him from worrying about whatever he was worrying about, she said, "Tell me more about your family. I don't really know anything about them."

"It's been such a while that I'm not sure I know anything about them, either." Miles sighed.

"Nonsense. You know all about them! You're clearly proud of them. What's your daughter's name?"

"Dana."

Myrtle said, "It's like pulling teeth getting information from you, Miles. Tell me about Dana. I'm curious." She sat down across from Miles in her armchair and tapped her fingers impatiently as she waited for Miles to gather his thoughts.

"She was our only child. Maeve's and mine." His voice was still tender when he said his wife's name, although it was many years since she'd passed away.

"What was Maeve like?" asked Myrtle, sensing an opening. She'd been curious for years about Miles's wife but she'd always felt he'd walled off Maeve in his memories.

"Fun-loving. Even zany sometimes."

Myrtle raised her eyebrows. "Opposites attracted, clearly."

"We were happy," he said simply. "She made everything better. We were very absorbed with each other, I think. Dana knew she was loved, but she knew her mom and I came first with each other."

"No other children?"

"We wanted others, but it wasn't to be. So we focused on Dana, when we weren't focusing on ourselves. Activities, support, all of those things you do for only children."

Myrtle said, "And I suppose Dana ditched it all to join a commune."

"What? No. She thrived on the attention she got. Learned three languages, studied abroad, went to law school."

Myrtle said, "Mm. A lawyer." Her tone wasn't particularly warm.

"At first. Then she went to medical school. She settled on medicine."

"She dropped out of law school?" asked Myrtle.

"No, she finished. She's both an attorney *and* a doctor."

"I sense a thread of over-achievement," said Myrtle.

"Yes. But she's still fun, like her mother was. And she's pretty laid-back. But she is very busy."

Myrtle said, "And the busyness keeps her from visiting."

"Yes. Well, it's not just that. She's a single mom, so she's doing everything. She married one of those tech guys in Silicon Valley. The marriage didn't work out, though," said Miles.

"When the marriage ended, I'd think Dana would have moved her family near you."

Miles shook his head. "No. She needed to stay in California so the kids could see their dad."

"Oh, I suppose that makes sense." Myrtle didn't know much about the nuts and bolts of divorce. "And how old are the kids now? They're teenagers. But what ages?"

Miles nodded. "Yes, they're teens." He looked down at the letter he was still clutching in his hand. "And I'm not *exactly* sure, although I should remember. I'm thinking they're fifteen and fourteen. But they might be sixteen and fifteen." This imprecision appeared to bother him, and he frowned at the letter.

"Well, you know what you need to do now, don't you?"

Miles glanced up from the letter, still frowning. "No."

"You need to call Dana. Tell her you're looking forward to seeing her. Does she mention the time of their flight? It'll take a couple of hours to drive from Charlotte. Are you picking them up?"

Miles looked startled by this idea. "She doesn't say."

Myrtle nodded. "Just as I said. The phone call."

Miles stood back up. "I think I'll call from home."

"Perfect. Just let me know how it all shakes out. And if you can still go with me tomorrow morning."

Now Miles was frowning again. "Go where?"

"To the yard sale, of course. Georgia is expecting us. As I mentioned, we'll be there early in the morning. You should have plenty of time to attend before your family arrives. Unless you're driving to Charlotte and back to meet an early flight, that is."

Miles, unable to handle the horrible uncertainty of the plans, hurried off to make his phone call. When he opened the front door, Pasha, Myrtle's feral cat, stared unblinkingly at him from the front step. Miles, wrapped up in his thoughts, jumped and yelped in a way that frightened Pasha just as much as she'd frightened him. Her back arched, and she hissed at him.

"Pasha!" called Myrtle. "Come on in, darling girl."

Pasha bounded in to Myrtle after giving Miles a reproachful glare and an angry swish of her tail. Miles, relieved, shut the door behind him.

There were no further interruptions that afternoon. Myrtle thought she'd be glad about this and at first, she was. Pasha curled up with her as she worked on her crossword. Then Myrtle spent some time reading—not the book club book, which she'd deemed unreadable, but something fun by Eudora Welty from a short story collection.

Around dinnertime, the phone rang. Myrtle smiled. She was now ready for interruptions because, at this point, there was nothing to interrupt.

"Elaine! How are you doing today?"

There was some happy crowing in the background, and Myrtle said, "And how is my brilliant grandson? I'm hearing happy sounds."

"Oh, he's doing great! He fingerpainted at preschool today and loved it. His clothes are multicolored now, but apparently the paint is supposed to come right off." Elaine paused. "Was there an incident with Red today? I saw the gnomes."

There was no way to avoid seeing the gnomes from Elaine and Red's perspective. They were front and center. Dusty had done an excellent job, despite working in a fifteen-minute time-frame. He must really have hustled—not an easy task at his age, and definitely not something ingrained in him.

"The same old thing, Elaine. You know."

Elaine said in a sympathetic tone. "Red was inserting himself into your business again."

"Yes. He was fretting about me not having my phone on me. Then he blew up when he realized I'd gotten rid of my landline."

Elaine said, "Ugh. And that followed right on the heels of his trip to the doctor with you."

"There are many indignities when you're an octogenarian," said Myrtle. "But Red somehow manages to be at the root of most of them."

"Well, I was going to invite you to come over to dinner," said Elaine, sighing. "But now I'm not sure it's a good idea."

Myrtle said, "Probably not. It might trigger more poor behavior from Red. Tell you what—why don't you drop Jack by here and you and Red have a nice quiet meal together? Maybe with candles."

"That's sweet of you! Especially considering you're not pleased with Red right now."

"Not at all," said Myrtle. "As always, I have an ulterior motive—spending time with Jack. Besides, it'll be nice for *you*. If Red has a pleasant evening, that's an unintended consequence."

So for a couple of hours, Jack and Myrtle played with trucks, airplanes, and a train. Then she read him a story about Thomas the Tank Engine until they both dozed off on the sofa. Elaine found them that way, snoring away, soon after. She quietly collected Jack, put a soft blanket over Myrtle, then locked the door behind her.

It was after one o'clock when Myrtle woke up again. Luckily, there was no crick in her neck. She rose from the sofa and stumbled into bed.

Two hours later, she was awake for the day. Myrtle sighed, staring at the ceiling and the bunny-shaped crack in it. The crack always put her in mind of the book *Goodnight Moon*. At one point in her life, she'd have identified with the bunny. Now, she supposed, she was the old woman whispering hush. To herself. She'd thought she might drift off for a little while longer, but then realized it was completely futile.

Myrtle peeked outside to see if the newspaper had miraculously arrived at three a.m. It hadn't. So she found her puzzle book and set about killing time with a cryptic crossword and a cup of coffee.

There was a tap on her door just thirty minutes later. She smiled. She'd wondered if Miles had also been stricken with insomnia. After all, he'd been reflecting on an unexpected visit from his family.

She opened the door and ushered Miles in. He was already dressed for the day in his usual khakis and button-down shirt. "No luck sleeping?" she asked.

He shook his head, looking exhausted. "No. I kept thinking of all the things I needed to do before the family arrives."

"Like what?"

"Cleaning. Grocery shopping. That sort of thing."

Myrtle frowned. "Miles, your house is always neat as a pin. And I thought you wanted to treat Dana and the boys to meals. Anyway, they're staying in a hotel, so they won't be eating breakfast with you."

"I want to make sure there are plenty of snacks there. Teenagers eat a lot, don't they?"

Myrtle said, "Red just about ate me out of house and home when he was a teenager. But they're not even staying with you long, are they?"

"A couple of nights."

"Then I wouldn't go overboard. I'll go to the store with you, if you like. I still think it might be fun if I have everybody over for dinner," said Myrtle.

"That won't be necessary," said Miles hastily. "At all."

"Okay, then I'll just help you brainstorm a list of snacks. It might help you relax to get this off your mind."

Myrtle pushed her puzzle aside, poured Miles coffee, and refreshed her cup, and they brainstormed a list of everything from cut up veggies in case the family was unexpectedly healthy ("She *is* a doctor," Miles had said), to cheese puffs in case they weren't.

"Did you find out if you're supposed to meet them at the airport?" asked Myrtle.

"Dana said they were renting a car. It's probably for the best. I've gotten too used to the poky traffic here in Bradley. When I lived in Atlanta, I didn't think twice about traffic jams or the speed people drove, but now I'm out of the habit."

Myrtle said darkly, "Yes. And they drive like crazy people in Charlotte."

Miles hid a smile. On the few occasions Myrtle drove, she always set out at a sedate twenty miles an hour.

"Now we just need to kill time until the yard sale. Then we can go to the store. After that, you'll be all ready for your family."

Miles was looking a little anxious again at the mention of his family, so Myrtle turned on the television. As usual, the only things on at three a.m. were nature shows, infomercials, and alarming news shows. They settled on the nature show.

"I never knew aardvarks were such interesting creatures," said Miles, sounding sleepy.

"I'm still not sure I find them all that interesting. I'm unconvinced. Hopefully, the next program will feature an animal with a bit more dynamism."

Then a show featuring sloths came on.

"There's got to be something else on," muttered Myrtle, wielding the remote. She settled on a disc golf competition.

"Is this a real sport?" asked Miles drowsily.

"Of course it is. Look, they have a scoring system and everything."

"They're playing with Frisbees," said Miles.

"It takes a good deal of skill. I don't think you and I could do it."

Miles considered this. "No, I suppose we couldn't. It's one of those things that looks easy enough, but isn't."

The phone rang, startling them both.

"Mercy," said Myrtle. "I hope it's not an emergency. It's only five o'clock."

Chapter Three

It was Georgia. "Myrtle. Knew you'd be up."

Myrtle frowned. "The yard sale hasn't started, has it?"

"Oh no. But you know how it is. The early birds will show up here at six, even though I made an eight o'clock start time. Is Miles over there?"

Myrtle said, "He sure is."

"Good. I'm a nervous wreck, waiting for this sale to kick off. Why don't the two of you come over and hang out? Help me kill time before everybody shows up."

Considering the alternative was watching disc golf, Myrtle agreed with alacrity. "Be right there."

Miles seemed to have woken up a bit. "Georgia needs help?"

"No. It sounds like she's all set up, but waiting is making her nervous."

Miles blinked. "I can't even imagine Georgia nervous. She's always so brash and confident."

"That's probably why she wants us over there. She's not used to feeling anxious, and she wants to fix the problem."

So Myrtle and Miles climbed into Miles's car. A few minutes later, they were at Georgia's house.

Georgia had been waiting and quickly ushered them in. She'd taken particular care over her appearance. Her normally unruly hair had been sprayed into compliance. She wore a dressy tank top that showed off her many tattoos and a nice pair of jeans. Her eyelashes were caked with mascara. So caked, in fact, that the lashes seemed unable to support the weight of it and were at half-mast.

Miles was always rather fascinated by Georgia. When she reached out unexpectedly to give them both a rough hug, he blushed.

"I really appreciate you two coming over here. I didn't sleep a wink last night and my stomach has felt like a roller coaster ever since I got up this morning. I need some distracting."

Myrtle said, "Say no more. Miles and I are up to the task."

"Good," said Georgia with relief. "I tried watching television but there was just some moronic stuff on there."

"We watched some educational shows on animals this morning," offered Miles.

Georgia quirked a drawn-on eyebrow. "Okay, so there were some things that *weren't* moronic on, I guess. But I wasn't in the mood to be educated. I wanted to be entertained."

They settled in Georgia's living room with the coffin coffee table, which Miles kept looking askance at. Although the house had allegedly been decluttered, it still appeared to be full of knickknacks and random clutter. Georgia plied them with more coffee. Myrtle had the feeling she was going to float away if she had more, but she gamely took it and started a monologue about the first thing that came into her head. That thing was Red and his interference.

Georgia was an attentive audience, laughing out loud at some points of the story. She said, "Got your gnomes out, I'm guessing?"

"Naturally. At least, as many as Dusty could pull out in fifteen minutes. He was on some sort of schedule."

Georgia seemed skeptical at the idea of Dusty being on any sort of schedule whatsoever. She said, "Well, at least you have a way of showing Red what you think of him getting into your business. The whole reason I'm having a yard sale is because my daughter told me my house was too cluttered and was an obstacle course." She snorted.

"I didn't even know you had a daughter," said Miles.

Georgia nodded. "I sure do. And she's a real smarty pants."

Myrtle said, "What have you put out for sale?"

Georgia chuckled. "Wanting to get a preview before the crowds show up?"

Miles gave Myrtle an alarmed look. He clearly wanted Georgia to realize that they were not planning on purchasing anything.

Myrtle hedged. "I'm just interested in hearing if you're planning on expanding your angel collection." It was a fib, of course, but Georgia happily took the bait. She was always ready to expound on her collection.

"Well, the truth of the matter is that I just plain love collecting the pretty little things. I like the *collecting* more than I even like looking at what I've got."

Miles frowned in confusion. "You mean the actual process?"

"Yep. Going to yard sales, thrift stores, looking online. I like the challenge of the hunt, I guess. But my daughter was right in some ways. I need to make more room if I'm going to expand my collection. So I have a few angels out there, Myrtle, in case you want to look at them."

For the next few minutes, Georgia regaled them with tales of her life, her points of view on practically everything, and followed up with a few salty jokes that made Miles blush again. Then she said, "Well, enough of this stuff. Let's eat."

She then proceeded to make them a surprisingly good repast of eggs, bacon, and hash browns. Even her coffee was good.

Once they'd finished that, Miles started looking drowsy again. Georgia gave her booming laugh and clapped her hands together, startling him. "No time for naps! We're about to be invaded."

"Are people really going to be arriving this early?" asked Miles, looking at his watch. "The sun isn't even up yet."

"You don't go to yard sales, do you?" asked Georgia with a snort.

Miles shook his head.

"Well, I go to tons of them. That's how I get all my collectibles, like I was saying." Georgia waved a hand around the room to indicate everything from the angels perched on every flat surface to the coffin, which, eerily, also held a slew of angels.

"And everyone shows up early?" asked Miles.

"Of course they do! You don't get the good stuff if you're not early. The early people are the *serious* people. They're people like me who want to add to specific collections. But they're also professionals—people who show up in pickup trucks and resell items online or at flea markets, or second-hand stores."

Miles frowned. "That doesn't sound particularly ethical. So they're reselling for a higher price than they're purchasing the item for?"

"Naturally. But let me tell you—the people hosting the sale are delighted to see them there. Because even though they're not making top dollar on the deal, they're making a lot more than they would if those dealers *weren't* there." Georgia looked at the clock. "We need to head out there."

So the three trudged outside. Georgia carefully locked the door behind her. She said grimly, "I've been reading articles about people robbing houses during yard sales."

Myrtle found this rather unlikely in Bradley. Although, she supposed, murders did seem to happen in her hometown on a regular basis. Robberies, not so much.

Georgia turned on her outdoor lights, illuminating the front yard and driveway. Myrtle saw that Georgia, despite the still-crowded appearance of her house, had gobs of things for sale. In fact, yard sale merchandise was everywhere. There were long tables holding lamps, vases, books, kitchen appliances, and VCR tapes. The ground was covered by odd chairs, small sofas, and other random furniture. She'd even strung up clothesline and had various rugs, comforters, quilts, and clothing hanging from them, forming aisles.

Miles blinked. Myrtle knew he must be thinking that his own home suddenly seemed a lot less cluttered than he'd thought.

It was fewer than five minutes before the first car pulled up in front of Georgia's house. Then there were several pickup trucks and more cars. Every shopper would walk through the yard with narrowed eyes, quickly evaluating the merchandise and, mostly, dismissing it.

Myrtle was about to think Georgia's yard sale was a complete bust when another truck pulled up. A slender man with dark hair and eyes and a rather cunning expression on his face got out.

Georgia sighed with relief. "I was hoping Victor would show up. Now I'm sure to get some sales."

But she wasn't going to have to wait for Victor. A shopper came up to her just then to haggle over the price of a set of dishes.

A familiar voice came from behind Myrtle and Miles. "Goodness. I didn't expect to see you two here."

It was Tippy Chambers. If Tippy had been surprised to see Myrtle and Miles, they were positively stunned to see Tippy there. Tippy was on the town council and lived in an immense house that was tastefully appointed in every way. She wore the finest of designer clothing. It seemed completely impossible that she would be interested in the bric-à-brac cluttering Georgia's yard.

"Good morning," said Myrtle. "We didn't expect to see you here, either."

Tippy smiled at her. "Well, you know. When I spoke with Georgia at book club, she seemed pretty nervous about the sale. I actually ran by yesterday evening to help her set up for today."

"Did you?" asked Miles. "I'd have been worried about tempting a rainstorm."

"Oh, Georgia was watching the forecast like a hawk. Plus, she just had so much stuff to sell that she was worried she couldn't pull it all out before the sale started if she waited until this morning."

"You're not shopping here then, I suppose?" asked Miles delicately.

Tippy said just as carefully, "Not today, no. I just wanted to come by and give Georgia some support. But it looks like it's going great. And you two are here, so I'll just say hi to Georgia and be on my way." She paused and looked at Myrtle. "Actually, I just remembered that I wanted to ask if you could help with passing out bulletins at church this Sunday. Melinda Merriweather can't make it, and I've had the dickens of a time getting a replacement for her."

Myrtle froze. Tippy had gotten savvier about recruiting Myrtle as a volunteer. It used to be that she could always tell when she was about to approach her because Tippy would square her shoulders and have this very determined expression on her face. But now, she didn't really have any tells at all. It was most discouraging.

Fortunately, Myrtle had an easy rejoinder. "I'm afraid I just can't. I've got a conflict." Myrtle had learned that it was best to be very vague, very firm, and to turn Tippy down right then. No checking calendars or letting her know later. If she procrastinated at all, Tippy would definitely rope her in.

Tippy sighed. "All right. Well, if you find you have some free time, let me know. You're coming to garden club, right?"

Myrtle nodded. She hadn't been in the mood to talk about plants, but her friend Wanda dearly loved going and she didn't want to disappoint her by not taking her along.

"I'd better go speak with Georgia. Y'all have a nice day."

Miles nodded courteously, and Myrtle gave Tippy a tight smile.

"That Tippy," muttered Myrtle as Tippy strode away.

"She's a very nice person," said Miles.

"Yes. That's precisely the problem. But I always suspect Red has reached out and asked her to keep me busy."

Miles said, "She probably thinks she's helping."

"Helping *Red*. He just wants to make sure I'm not meddling. And that I'm wrapped in cotton wool to ensure I live another twenty years."

Miles, although too polite to say anything, looked rather shocked at the mention of twenty years.

"It's very possible, Miles. I have tough genes and a resilient constitution. Twenty years is entirely plausible, even though I'm in my mid-eighties." She stretched. "But I'll thank you not to bring up such delicate topics."

Miles opened his mouth, but no words dared emerge.

"Let's do a walk-through of Georgia's sale. Then we can go to the store and make sure you have plenty of goodies for your family's visit."

So they proceeded on a very odd tour. There were cans of tennis balls (Myrtle was quite certain Georgia had never played the sport), a glow-in-the-dark portrait of Elvis done in velvet, a basket full of unused toothbrushes, and some very peculiar Christmas tree ornaments.

Miles shivered. "Isn't it about time we left?" He kept his voice low. "This stuff is giving me the creeps."

"You're so sensitive, Miles! It's just yard sale merchandise. I can certainly see why Georgia wanted to get rid of some of this stuff."

"No, really. I'm getting a bad vibe here."

Myrtle frowned. "I don't remember you being particularly clairvoyant. That was always the provenance of your cousin Wanda."

Miles shivered again, although it was unclear whether he was shivering at the fey feeling he was experiencing or at being compared to Wanda.

"Okay, we'll head out. I just want to see the other side of this rug. If it's unstained, perhaps I could buy it for my kitchen."

Miles looked exasperated. "I thought we'd agreed we were not going to shop here. If you get something and I don't, it's going to look like I don't like Georgia's things."

"You *don't* like Georgia's things. Anyway, the rug is cute."

Miles shook his head. "You know how Red is about area rugs. He thinks they're tripping hazards."

"I'll use two-sided tape to tack it down. Besides, I've heard enough about what Red thinks. He's gotten entirely too involved in my business."

So Myrtle rounded the corner of the hanging rug and saw, not an unstained second side, but a body lying on the ground.

Chapter Four

Myrtle drew in a hissing breath. She reached down gingerly to put her hand on the side of the man's neck to check for a pulse. "He's gone," she said grimly.

They stared down at the man. Myrtle realized it was Victor, the man Georgia had been so excited to see arriving at the sale. At first, she wondered if he could have been struck down naturally by a stroke or an aneurism or a heart attack. Scattered around Victor were an angel and a couple of other yard sale items.

Miles sounded somber. "You're sure he's gone?"

Myrtle nodded. "I suppose we'll have to call Red." She didn't seem to relish the idea.

"I'll call him," said Miles, pulling his phone out of the pocket of his khaki pants.

Myrtle glanced around more carefully as Miles made the call. It was then that she noticed the wrought iron yard art lying slightly under the edge of the rug. It appeared to have blood on the base.

Then there was a blood-curdling shriek, as if someone was being murdered just feet away. They spun around. An older woman had dropped a basket of yard sale finds and was screaming bloody murder. Now others were running over and talking loudly.

Miles, still trying to speak with Red, was saying, "Yes, we're all fine. People are just upset." He put his hand over his other ear to block out the noise and walked away from the body.

Myrtle glowered at everyone and bellowed, "Everybody must step *back*. Immediately! The authorities are on their way." At least, they better be. Otherwise, this was one crime scene that was going to spiral out of control.

Everyone but the older woman obediently moved away, muttering as they did so. The older woman, however, appeared to have grown roots and was planted where she stood. Myrtle hissed at her, "Move away! Get back to the street!"

The woman just blinked at her.

Heaving a long-suffering sigh, Myrtle stalked toward her, put an arm around her, and moved her along, still holding her cane in her other hand.

"Now, you'll be just fine," said Myrtle in a voice that brooked no argument. "Let's find Georgia and get you a glass of ice water."

"Who's Georgia?" asked the woman faintly.

"The person holding this yard sale you're attending."

The woman said, "Okay. It's just that I'm at an age where shocks like this are hard for me."

Myrtle rolled her eyes. "You're young enough to be my daughter. Look, here's Georgia."

And indeed it was—a very confused Georgia who wasn't sure why her merchandise had elicited such an outcry from the shoppers.

Myrtle swiftly explained what had happened, handed her charge over to Georgia, and scurried back to Victor to guard the scene until Red could arrive.

Miles joined her. "He's coming." He looked down at the man. "Pity. He's fairly young, too. I suppose it must have been a heart attack or some such."

"It was nothing of the sort," said Myrtle crisply. "He was murdered. The weapon is right there."

Miles's eyes opened wide.

"We'll protect the scene until Red gets here. And make sure no one leaves so Red can collect witness statements."

Miles seemed eager to leave the proximity of the body. "I'll let the others know they need to wait around."

That suited Myrtle just fine. She stayed exactly where she was, making sure no one trampled the crime scene. She was just as quiet as Victor and about as still as she waited.

It wasn't long before Red arrived. Even though he was obscured by the rug and the quilts hanging next to it, she could see his big shoes approaching. Stomping, actually.

Sure enough, his face soon peered around the textiles. His face was just as florid as his hair was. "Mama! What are you doing?"

She calmly said, "I'm protecting a crime scene. What are *you* doing?"

"Did you touch anything?"

"Yes. I carefully touched his neck to make sure he was dead and didn't require an ambulance. That's all I touched."

Red backed her out of the area and pointed to Georgia's house. "I need you to go inside now. Sit with Georgia until after I can speak with you."

Myrtle nodded and headed for the house while Red announced to the gathered yard sale shoppers that everyone needed to stay on the premises but in their cars.

Georgia and Miles turned as she came in. Georgia was slumped at her kitchen table, looking glum. The older woman had, fortunately, gone back to her car to wait to speak with Red.

Myrtle said, "You all right, Georgia?"

"Not a bit. Miles told me that this guy was murdered."

"I'm afraid so," said Myrtle. "Did you know him?"

"Not well, no. I was glad he was here at first because he's one of those guys who buys up stuff and sells it on the internet. But I had words with him probably thirty minutes ago. He called my stuff tacky." Georgia looked very indignant at this. She peered at Myrtle. "What was the murder weapon? I didn't hear a gun go off, and surely we'd have heard something if a grown man was killed with a knife."

Miles looked uncomfortable. Myrtle also felt a bit awkward. It wasn't very nice telling someone that their yard art had been weaponized. Besides, she imagined the police would want to keep the method under wraps.

"It looked as if he might have been hit on the head with something," she said vaguely.

Georgia now looked rather crushed. "It wasn't something the killer found at the yard sale, was it?"

Myrtle said, "I'm not really sure, Georgia. It was quite chaotic out there. What can you tell me about Victor?"

"He's Victor Fowler. He's technically a neighbor. He became separated from his wife, Jo, not too long ago."

Myrtle and Miles looked at each other. A separated wife sounded like a plausible suspect.

"Was their split acrimonious?" asked Myrtle.

Georgia snorted. "Myrtle. You're talking to *me*. Plain English, please."

"Was the split friendly?" amended Myrtle.

"Well, you know I don't really spend a lot of time listening to tittle-tattle. But from what I understood, Jo was hoping to get back together with Victor. Although, from what I understand, both Victor and Jo were seeing people outside their marriage."

Right then, there was a strangled scream outside. They leaped to their feet.

"Not another body," growled Georgia. "Not in my yard!"

"It's probably that obnoxious woman again," muttered Myrtle.

But it wasn't. When Georgia exploded out the door, Red was there with an attractive woman with sandy hair and blue eyes. Those blue eyes had tears streaming from them and the woman's expression was shocked.

Red said grimly, "Georgia, do you mind hosting Jo Fowler for a minute?"

Myrtle could see that there was a crowd of people gawking at Jo and Red from the road.

"Course not," said Georgia, ushering the woman inside.

She settled Jo into a chair at the kitchen table and proceeded to swiftly give her both a glass of water and a glass of whiskey in rapid succession.

Myrtle wondered if Jo perhaps thought it too early in the day to drink whiskey, but she quaffed it at once, absently drying her mouth with the back of her hand. She looked pleadingly at the three of them. "What happened? Is it true? Is Victor gone?"

Georgia and Miles looked at Myrtle, hoping she'd step in as spokesperson.

Myrtle felt it was best to come right out with bad news, just like ripping off a bandage. "I'm afraid so. It appears he was murdered."

"Murdered." Jo sank back into the wooden chair.

"How did you end up here at the yard sale?" asked Myrtle. "Were you here to shop? Or were you here to see Victor?"

At Victor's name, Jo crumpled up again. Myrtle hastily pulled out a clean tissue from a packet she kept in her large purse. She couldn't abide tears, although she understood this might be an occasion that warranted them.

Jo finally croaked, "I figured he'd be here. He went to all the yard sales. I'd been trying to reach out to him, but he hadn't been answering my calls. I just wanted the chance to speak with him."

"Did you have to drive a long way?" asked Myrtle.

Jo shook her head. "I'm renting a place down the road." She buried her face in her hands. "I should have come earlier. I figured he'd be here, and he'd arrive early. Maybe, if I'd shown up, this wouldn't have happened."

"Now, there's no reason to blame yourself," said Georgia stoutly. "The only person to blame is the one who did this."

"You were at home all morning, then?" asked Myrtle, trying to sound casual and not as if she was looking for Jo's alibi.

Jo nodded. "Victor and I are separated, and I haven't been able to sleep a wink since I moved out. I slept in this morning because I'd been tossing and turning all night last night. I'd been feeling pretty down lately and had a tough time facing my days. Depression, apparently."

"You're seeing a doctor about that, right?" asked Georgia.

Jo shook her head. "I thought it would all be resolved once Victor and I were back together. And we were sure to reconcile." She sobbed. "We were meant to be together . . . soulmates."

Myrtle fished out the entire packet of tissues this time and shoved it at Jo. "Do you have any idea who might have done this?"

Jo's face darkened. She nodded. "I saw Millicent out there."

Georgia lifted her penciled-on eyebrows. "Mmm."

Miles cleared his throat. "Who is Millicent?"

"Millicent Montgomery," said Georgia. "She wasn't real happy with Victor."

Jo gave a derisive snort. "That's one way of putting it. She's an amateur yard sale shopper. Victor used to say she was like a magpie. She always went for bright, shiny objects. But the problem was that she didn't spend any time researching stuff. Victor, on the other hand, *he* knew what would sell. He knew the true value of things because he looked them up. It used to drive me crazy—he'd tune out the entire world and spend hours on his laptop, making notes."

"But Millicent didn't?" asked Myrtle.

"Too lazy. So instead, she took a shortcut. She'd follow Victor around at different yard sales to see what he was looking at. Anything he paid any sort of attention to, she'd swoop in and get."

Miles said, "I'm sorry, but I just don't totally understand. Victor and Millicent were going to yard sales, scoping out the inventory, and then reselling the items? Where?"

"Online," said Jo simply.

"And you can make good money doing that?" asked Miles.

"Oh yes. Victor made a small fortune. But he knew what he was doing. Like I said, that's why Millicent was shadowing him."

Myrtle frowned. "But you seemed to intimate that Millicent might have had a motive for murder. Why would she murder the person who was inadvertently helping her out?"

Georgia murmured, "English, Myrtle."

But Jo understood what she was asking. "Oh, Victor told me all about it. Millicent had a yard sale of her own, and Victor discovered something valuable there. A first edition James Bond novel. It was even signed. Victor bought it for a dollar and sold it for a real bundle to a collector. Millicent didn't take too kindly over that."

The door flew open and Red was there, looking sweaty and his face even more florid. "Jo? Could I speak with you for a few minutes?"

Jo rose, nodding. Red looked at Myrtle and Miles. "I'm going to need to speak with the two of you next, so if you could continue hanging out for a while, that would be great."

Which was fine, except Myrtle was itching to find out what was going on outside. She stood up from the kitchen table and strode over to a window.

Georgia sighed. "Guess I'm going to have to call off the yard sale. The place is a crime scene now."

Miles asked her, "Were you able to sell much? Before, I mean."

Georgia shook her head, looking chipper. "Nope. I figured Victor was going to grab a lot of stuff, but he never got the chance. Now I can tell my daughter that I tried to have a yard sale, but that fate got in the way."

"It's nice to find a bright side," said Miles, sounding as if he wasn't sure repopulating Georgia's house with all her knick-knacks was indeed a bright side.

Myrtle said absently, "You could always reschedule it. You've got price stickers on everything already." She looked out at the people in Georgia's yard.

"What's going on out there, Myrtle?" asked Georgia idly.

"Well, there are a lot of gaping people staring at your yard, as one would expect. Red is speaking with Jo, who looks very emotional."

Then she spotted a large man with a receding hairline. The man was carrying a notebook.

Myrtle said, "Sloan! What's he doing here?"

"Probably reporting," said Miles.

"*I'm* his crime reporter! Plus, I found the body." She spent the next thirty seconds hammering on the window and making shooing gestures. "Is he deaf?" asked Myrtle in exasperation.

Red was not deaf, apparently, and shot his mother a very annoyed look. Sloan, however, continued looking blissfully unaware.

Finally, with more window hammering, the newspaper editor glanced up at the source of the racket. Seeing Myrtle there, he winced. Myrtle had been his high school English teacher, from which he'd never recovered. He gave her a weak wave. Myrtle replied with more shooing gestures, some emphatic enough that they nearly bowled her over. She was relieved to see Sloan slink away.

Chapter Five

"This whole thing is pretty sad. Jo sounded so sure that she and Victor would get back together again," said Georgia.

"Were they well-suited?" asked Miles.

"Not a bit. They'd yell at each other all the time. I reckon it was their love language, though."

Myrtle continued peering out the window now that Sloan was safely driving away. "Now Jo is pointing at Millicent and raising her voice."

She quickly opened the window just in time to hear Jo screaming, "You did it. You've been following Victor around. Stalking him at all the yard sales. You were furious with him about selling your stupid book."

Millicent, however, quickly turned the tables. "*You're* the one who's been stalking Victor. You think I haven't noticed? You've been following him everywhere!"

"I was just trying to get back with him!" sobbed Jo.

"This sounds very much like the last episode of *Tomorrow's Promise*," murmured Myrtle.

Red seemed torn between shooing away gaping onlookers, and listening to hear what information the women might divulge next.

Millicent stomped away. Red called after her, "Millicent? I need you to stick around, please. I want to speak with you."

Myrtle closed the window.

Miles, who'd already been looking glum, was now looking anxious. "It sounds like Red has a long list of people he needs to speak with. I've really got to get ready for my family's visit."

"Family?" Georgia raised her eyebrows. "I never realized you had any, Miles. Where've you been hiding them?"

"They're simply very busy on the west coast," said Miles, sounding prickly. "But they're coming this afternoon. I need to get to the grocery store to buy a few things ahead of their arrival."

Georgia gestured to the clock on the wall. The clock was, in itself, interesting. It had numbers, out of order, splashed all over the face. It was reminiscent of Dali's work without Dali's flair. "It's still very early in the morning. You've got plenty of time."

Miles stared at the clock. "How on earth do you tell time on that?"

"Oh, you get used to it," said Georgia with a shrug. "Okay, looks like I need to come up with a distraction until Red talks to us. How about a game of poker?"

Myrtle thought poker was a most uncouth game. She'd have preferred canasta. In terms of a distraction, however, she thought it could serve a purpose.

For the next thirty minutes, the three were engaged in a card game. Georgia, sadly, was an excellent card player. Her poker face was completely inscrutable. Miles, on the other hand, looked startled when he got a bad hand. Myrtle was somewhere between the two.

Finally, Red returned. "Mama? Miles?"

Georgia said, "You can talk to them here in the kitchen, if you want. I'll head to the back for a few."

Red sat at the table with them, pushing some cards out of the way so that he could set his notebook down. He rubbed his face. "Okay. How did this all come about?"

"Organically, Red, as per usual. We certainly didn't *plan* on discovering a body today," said Myrtle crisply.

"Right. Although it seems to be a particular talent of yours."

"One must have *some* talents," said Myrtle.

Red looked at his mother as if not entirely sure if she were casting aspersions on him or not. He turned to Miles. "How did the two of you end up here? I don't think of you as being a yard sale kind of guy, Miles."

Miles looked pleased at that. "No, I don't suppose I am. But we're friends of Georgia's, of course, and Georgia was anxious about the yard sale. She wanted to kill time before it started. She gave your mother a call this morning."

"At the crack of dawn?" asked Red.

"Oh, dawn hadn't cracked yet," said Myrtle.

"And yet you were up and ready for the day."

"Naturally. Miles was over visiting, and Georgia extended the invitation to him, too. We came over and chatted for a bit. Then, once people started arriving, Miles and I walked around to see what sort of merchandise Georgia had available."

"And you found Victor," said Red.

Myrtle nodded. "That's right."

Red rubbed his face. "Okay. What are you doing the rest of the day?"

"Well, we're certainly not going gallivanting around discovering other bodies," said Myrtle severely. "Miles has family coming in."

"Family?" Red looked more surprised at this than the fact his mother had discovered a body at a yard sale.

Miles nodded. "My daughter and grandsons."

"Isn't that something?" said Red, sounding amazed. "Well, then. You'll have to bring them by." He stood up from the table. "You two are free to go. Enjoy your family time."

Red walked out. Myrtle called out to Georgia to let her know they were leaving, and then she and Miles headed to his car.

"Everyone seems very surprised about my family," said Miles as he drove them away from Georgia's house.

"Well, you have to admit that it's pretty remarkable. I was thinking your family was entirely imaginary."

Miles said, "Inventing an imaginary family sounds like something a deranged person might do."

"When one doesn't offer proof of a family, the family seems a bit doubtful."

"But I do have proof, Myrtle! I have a picture up on my desk in my living room."

"That little thing?" scoffed Myrtle. "You could have created that with photo software using strangers from the internet."

Miles sighed. "Well, they do actually exist. And they'll be coming over sooner rather than later. Shall we head to the store? Or should I run back home first and clean up?"

"Considering there's nothing to clean, I think the wiser course of action would be to grocery shop."

Fifteen minutes later, they were in the Piggly-Wiggly. Miles was moving slowly through the grocery store due to a tremendous amount of indecision.

"For heaven's sake. It won't matter what type of crackers you put out, Miles."

Miles wasn't so sure. "They shouldn't make so many choices available. It's overwhelming."

Myrtle plucked one a box off the shelf. "There. Problem solved. Let's move on."

Miles frowned at the package. "I want to say that one of my grandchildren eats gluten-free things."

"Then get some gluten-free crackers as well. It's not brain surgery."

Miles was then totally absorbed in the varieties of gluten-free crackers. "Some of them appear to be corn based. Some are rice based. And a few have potatoes in them."

"Potatoes," said Myrtle.

"Do those taste better?"

"Who knows? I'm just trying to move on to the next aisle. If we don't get this show on the road, your family will be on your doorstep, and we'll still be at the grocery store."

Thirty minutes later, they finally finished. Miles drove them back. He was about to pull into Myrtle's driveway when she said, "I'll give you a hand putting these things away. Or setting some of them out."

Miles looked relieved. "Would you? I have the terrible feeling I'm going to obsess over every detail."

"Which is precisely why I offered. Your family is coming to see *you*. They're not coming to check out your charcuterie tray."

Miles frowned again. "I don't have a charcuterie tray."

"Put it all on a cutting board."

Miles frowned. "The cutting board is sort of disreputable-looking. I've done a lot of cutting on it."

"You can borrow mine, if you like."

Miles raised an eyebrow. "You have a charcuterie tray?"

"You act as if I'm some sort of savage, Miles! I certainly do. It's from the 1950s."

"Did people eat charcuterie then?"

Myrtle said, "It's technically a relish tray. Sort of a lazy Susan thing. But I repurposed it. Anyway, I'll be back out in a snap."

So Miles did drive into Myrtle's driveway. She reappeared shortly thereafter bearing the relish tray.

"That looks fancy," said Miles, seeming uncomfortable.

"It's crystal."

"I wouldn't want them to think I'm trying too hard," said Miles.

"You *are* trying too hard. You might as well show it. Now let's get started."

A few minutes later, they were at Miles's house in his kitchen. Myrtle dumped some olives into the center of the lazy Susan. Then she sliced cheese and put the charcuterie on the tray. "There. Perfect."

"What about the chips? Should we put them in baskets or something?"

Myrtle shook her head. "Then they won't know the flavors of each one. Now, let's talk about something else. You're entirely too wound up about this visit."

"Let me guess what you want to talk about."

"Victor's murder. You're exactly right. But let's face it, Miles. It's up to us to figure out what's going on. Red is hopeless at this stuff," said Myrtle.

"Red is a very capable police officer," said Miles.

"Yes, when it's a matter of sorting out the teenagers who spray-painted Mrs. Oleander's garbage can. But when it comes to the big things, he's less competent. Anyway, back to the original point. I believe we should speak with Millicent Montgomery just as soon as we can. I'm imagining you'll have some free time since your family isn't going to be staying at the house with you."

Miles frowned at her. "I can hardly tell them I'm running off to investigate a murder."

"But you *have* told them we've put a number of dangerous people behind bars, haven't you? Because that's something to be proud of."

Miles muttered something under his breath.

"Besides, you won't have to say a thing. If there are two teenagers in your family, the days won't be starting early. They're apt to play video games on their phones until three in the morning and then sleep past noon. You'll have lots of time."

Miles looked rather glum at this. Whether at the prospect of investigating a murder or at his grandsons playing video games until all hours, it was difficult to determine.

"I'm not saying, of course, that Millicent is definitely the killer, just because I want to see her. But it sounds as if she might hold a grudge against Victor for having made money off that book at her yard sale."

Miles said, "I don't understand her bad feelings at Victor at all. That's part and parcel of selling things, isn't it? One man's junk is another man's treasure. Aren't there entire television shows devoted to the value of things that were perceived as rubbish?"

"I suppose you're referring to *Antique Roadshow*. But not all of those things are picked up from yard sales and not all of them are perceived as junk. Sometimes people think their belongings are priceless and they end up being some sort of mass-produced knick-knack."

Miles said, "But sometimes it's exactly the opposite. Which is apparently what happened in Millicent's case. It seems there should be a Latin phrase for it. All I can come up with is caveat emptor, which won't work."

"It's 'caveat subscriptor' when the *seller* is the one who needs to beware."

Miles raised his eyebrows. "You're quite a treasure trove of Latin phrases."

"Yes," agreed Myrtle smugly. "Anyway, it seems Millicent didn't beware at all. I think she must have been horrified that Victor made a killing off of something she didn't realize was valuable. She was probably just wanting to clear out her bookshelves and didn't look twice at the Ian Fleming book. I'm not sure if that's enough for her to want to commit murder, however."

"What about Jo?"

"Victor's loving ex-wife?" asked Myrtle. "I have to wonder if she was quite as eager to get back together with Victor as it appeared. Maybe she harbored some long-simmering resentment over his treatment of her. She saw her opportunity and killed him with the flamingo."

"Now that's definitely an example of caveat emptor. Except the buyer didn't realize he had to beware of the flamingo."

Myrtle nodded. "But what if we took Jo at her word? What if she *did* genuinely want to get back together with Victor? She was separated from him, but was longing to mend their marriage. But then Victor started seeing someone."

Miles said, "Wouldn't that mean she'd want to kill the woman Victor was seeing? Instead of Victor himself?"

"Perhaps not. Maybe she viewed Victor's perfidy as real treachery. He deserted her. He started rekindling his love for someone else."

Miles tilted his head to one side. "I believe you've watched too many soap operas." He glanced from the kitchen across his living room and frowned. Grabbing a brightly colored microfiber cloth from under the kitchen sink, he swooped down to eliminate a few specks of dust that had the temerity to settle there.

Myrtle rolled her eyes. "You'll have a lot in common with your grandkids. They'll be shooting video game monsters, and you'll be zapping dust particles."

The doorbell suddenly rang. Miles froze.

"It can't be them," he whispered. "I'm not ready yet."

"For heaven's sake, Miles. You were ready even before we went shopping. I saw the inside of your fridge, remember? My advice to you is to get rid of your perfectionist tendencies, at least during the course of this visit."

Miles was, however, still frozen. Myrtle strode over to his front door and yanked it open just as the doorbell rang again.

"Hello there!" said Myrtle brightly, to several very nice-looking people on Miles's doorstep. "I'm Myrtle, a friend of Miles's. Please come inside!"

"Oh, you're the marvelous Myrtle," said a tall woman with sparkling blue eyes and dimples. "I've heard all about you."

Myrtle stepped aside to let them in. "If you've heard I'm marvelous, it's all true." She was about to introduce Miles to his own family when she stopped. "Well, then, I should be on my way."

"Why not stay for just a few minutes, Myrtle?" asked Miles.

"Yes, visit for a while," said the woman. "I'm Dana, by the way, although I think you've already figured that out."

"Especially since she's a detective," said the younger of the two teenagers, looking somewhat interested.

The boys were tall as well. They had thick, brown hair that flopped over their foreheads and into their eyes. Myrtle, who was excellent at summing up teens based on her many years of school teaching, found them to be alert and intelligent. Especially the one who mentioned her detective work.

"Here are Ben and Ethan," said Dana, looking proud.

Miles gave them all a hug and stepped aside. "Was the trip all right?" he asked anxiously. "I know it was a long way to drive."

"Oh, we played games along the way," said Ethan, the older boy, with a smile.

"The license plate game? Counting cows?" asked Myrtle.

The boys looked blankly at Myrtle. "Video games on our phones," offered Ben.

"Oh, right," said Myrtle as she fell into the generation gap between them.

Ben, the younger boy, gave her a sympathetic smile.

Miles quickly said, "You must be ready for something to eat. That was a long drive from Charlotte. I have snacks."

The boys' eyes lit up at the mention of snacks.

Dana said, "That would be great. We grabbed something at the airport, but the boys are probably ready for something else."

Miles pulled out the snacks, beautifully arranged on Myrtle's ancient relish tray. They watched as the food was quickly decimated.

Dana gave Myrtle and Miles a rueful look. "Boys."

Myrtle said, "At least it's clear that they're *enjoying* the food. It would be bad if they'd turned their noses up at it."

"No way they'd have done that. They'll eat anything." She looked at Miles with concern. "Are you okay, Dad? You're looking tired."

Miles opened his eyes wide, as if caught doing something untoward. "Am I? I can't imagine why."

Myrtle raised an eyebrow at him. "Can't you?"

Miles gave her a stern look. He apparently didn't want to bring up murder. At least not this early in his family's visit.

But Dana was catching on that something had happened. "Is something wrong? You don't have any health problems, right?" She was now looking her father up and down with a piercing gaze, as if she could see what he might be suffering from just by staring at him. Which, considering she was a physician, she probably could.

"Nothing like that," said Miles hurriedly. "Nothing to do with me. Myrtle and I just had something of an adventure this morning. Unexpectedly."

Ben looked up from the tray. "Did someone get murdered?" His eyes were wide.

Dana chuckled. "You act like that's an everyday occurrence, Ben. I'm sure something else must have happened."

Miles and Myrtle stared at each other.

Dana's eyes grew enormous. "*Was* it murder?"

"It was, actually. It was no one we were close with, and we weren't in any danger," said Miles quickly.

"Okay, we're going to want to hear all about that," said Dana. She sat down on the sofa, and they all settled in various chairs, looking eagerly at Miles.

"Why don't you tell the story, Myrtle?" asked Miles.

Miles was never a fan of being the center of attention. For a moment, Myrtle briefly debated whether she should make him tell the story and let him be the hero. But then, looking at his face, she decided he really *didn't* want to tell it. Plus, he might very well botch the story entirely, which Myrtle certainly wouldn't do.

So she told the whole thing. The lead-up to the yard sale (Dana stopped her momentarily to inquire if Miles really *didn't* sleep often), the trip to Georgia's, their little tour of Georgia's assembled oddities, the horrid discovery of poor Victor, the obnoxious onlookers, Red's irritated arrival, and their being questioned. Miles's family was enthralled.

"So what will you do now?" asked Ben, looking at Myrtle and his grandfather with interest.

Ethan, the older boy, snorted. "What do you mean, 'what are they going to do?' They're going to let the cops figure out what's going on."

"Is that right?" asked Dana. "Is that what you'll do? Or are you going to poke around some?"

Myrtle said, "Well, I for one plan on being a little nosy. After all, I'm a crime reporter for the town newspaper. As soon as I leave here, I'm checking in with my editor and writing a story. Miles, on the other hand, will have a lovely visit with all of you. He was really excited to hear you were coming."

It was a bit of an embellishment. Miles had been *agitated* about them coming. That could, she supposed, translate into excitement.

She thought Dana looked more relaxed at this. She looked like the kind of person who didn't necessarily want a senior citizen father to be involved in crime fighting.

Dana said, "We've been excited to see him, too."

Miles looked anxious again. "I'm afraid it's not so exciting of a place. When you visited me in Atlanta, we had plenty of entertainment options. Here in Bradley, there are . . . fewer."

Myrtle looked rather indignant, apparently forgetting that she was frequently bored in her town. "Now, Miles! We have plenty of things to do."

Dana quickly interjected, "Besides, we're not here to do things. We're here to visit with you, Dad."

"And investigate a murder," said Ben, his eyes gleaming.

"We're doing no such thing," said Dana sternly.

They chatted a few more minutes. Myrtle asked after the boys' school. She knew it was a lame question that the teens probably were tired of answering, but having been a schoolteacher, it was what she was most interested in. Both boys apparently took after their grandfather and were in advanced science and math classes. Ben was also good in English class, although Ethan was less-interested.

Myrtle gave them all a smile and stood up. "Well, it's been lovely meeting you all. I told Miles to bring you over and let me cook you supper, actually."

Miles looked suddenly extremely agitated. Dana seemed to hide a smile.

"But then he said something about taking you out to eat, so I suppose he's made plans. Anyway, I'm sure I'll see you later on."

With that, she told them all goodbye and took her leave.

Chapter Six

A few minutes later, she was back at her own house. She turned on her laptop, and then pulled out her cell phone to call Sloan Jones, her editor at the newspaper. Myrtle sincerely hoped he'd ditched his lame attempt to cover the murder du jour.

Sloan answered, sounding nervous. "Miss Myrtle?"

"Hi Sloan. You haven't been working on that yard sale homicide, have you?"

"As a matter of fact, I have, Miss Myrtle," said Sloan, the words spilling out on top of each other. "Red asked me to when I saw him there."

"Interesting," said Myrtle crisply. "I was under the impression that Red worked for the police department, not the *Bradley Bugle*."

"Uhhh."

"As it happens, I'll write a much more coherent piece for the paper than you will. And I know you care more about the newspaper's content than you do about pleasing Red Clover. At least, that's what I assumed. I've always considered you a professional, Sloan. I'll write a better article." This, again, was something of an embellishment. Myrtle crossed her fingers at the fib.

"Do you have some inside information about what happened?" asked Sloan. "Is that what you mean about you writing a better article?"

Myrtle actually meant that she was, by far, a better writer than Sloan was. After all, she'd marked up his papers in English class. But she diplomatically said, "That's exactly right. Miles and I were the ones who discovered the victim, after all."

"And you know who the victim was?" Now Sloan sounded less anxious and more interested.

"I sure do. Was Red withholding that information?"

"That's right. But he said it was because he had to notify the family first," said Sloan.

"Naturally. We wouldn't want them to find out about his death from reading the newspaper, would we? Tell you what. I know Lieutenant Perkins from the state police. He's ordinarily the one who partners with Red on homicides. I'll ask him if the victim's family has been notified before I write the story."

Sloan paused. "You know how to get in touch with Perkins?"

"I have his cell phone number." Myrtle sounded smug.

"All right, then. It makes sense for you to write the story, I suppose. Just—tell Red it was all your idea."

"Of course," said Myrtle huffily. "It's not as if we don't go through this every single time, Sloan. I should simply tape record these tedious conversations of ours and play them back whenever we're inevitably in the same situation."

She rang off and searched her contacts list for Lieutenant Perkins. She was very fond of Perkins. He was much more deferential than her son was. Plus, he was often more forthcoming.

He picked up immediately. "Mrs. Clover," he said. "What a pleasure. How are you doing?"

"Oh, pretty well, Lt. Perkins. Of course, I had something of an exciting morning."

"I heard about that," said Perkins. "You were in the thick of it all, as usual."

"Yes. It does always seem that way. I know you must be very busy right now, but I did want to ask you the quickest of questions. It seems my newspaper editor was warned not to name the victim because the family hadn't yet been notified. Can I assume that the family has been informed before the paper comes out tomorrow morning? Or should I leave the victim's name out?"

"That's very thoughtful of you to ask, Mrs. Clover."

Myrtle preened.

"The family has indeed been notified. The members who don't live in town had their local police inform them of the tragedy. The police reported back that it had all been handled. Locally, Red and I personally visited the family member."

Myrtle said, "I see. Perfect. Then I will run Victor's name in tomorrow's edition." She paused. "While I have you on the phone, might I ask you something else?"

Now Perkins' voice was wary, although it retained its customary politeness. "You're always welcome to ask."

"Are you investigating any particular leads? Were you able to gather any evidence from the crime scene, for example?"

Perkins said cautiously, "I'm afraid I can't go into the details, although we found some footprints in the soil that we're planning on checking out. Unfortunately, the scene already had quite a few people walking through it, of course."

"Any DNA? Or fibers?" asked Myrtle sweetly.

"There might be some DNA and some fiber evidence we're pursuing," said Perkins rather evasively.

"Mm. To me, the oddest thing about this murder is the location of the crime. Thinking along those lines, what type of person do you think might have done something like this in such a public place? Any ideas?"

"None for publication, sadly."

"Mm," said Myrtle again. "It seemed to me that it would be reasonable that someone who murders someone else at a yard sale is the type of individual who is overconfident or very desperate. Would you agree with that assessment?"

Always the diplomat, Perkins said, "It does certainly make sense, although I can't comment on it in any official capacity, Mrs. Clover."

Then there was a loud voice in the background on Perkins's end of the line. "Are you speaking to my mother, Perkins?"

Myrtle sighed.

Sure enough, Red quickly took the phone away from the lieutenant. "Mama! Why are you pestering Perkins? He has an important job to do."

"Because *I* have an important job to do. I'm reporting this story for the paper."

"No, you're not. Sloan is. He told me so," said Red.

"Well, he quickly capitulated when I told him I discovered the victim. And I wasn't pressing Perkins for details," said Myrtle, crossing her fingers again at the lie. "I was merely trying to glean what information I responsibly could include in my article."

"I'm guessing you got that," said Red. It sounded as if he were speaking through gritted teeth.

"I did indeed. Perkins is always most helpful."

"Good. Now you need to focus on writing your story and not get involved in this case in any way. Watch your soap opera. Reorganize your gnome collection. Replace the batteries in your remote. I'm sure you can find something innocuous to do." And with that, Red ended the phone call.

Myrtle fumed. Dusty would need to add more gnomes to the ones that were already facing Red's house. Red was being completely incorrigible. He was even worse than usual, and that was difficult to imagine.

There was a knock at Myrtle's door, and she frowned. She had the terrible sensation it might be her ghastly neighbor, Erma Sherman. Myrtle had been feeling very lucky not to have had a recent Erma encounter. She might have jinxed herself. Myrtle was loath to go to the door in case Erma spotted her.

Then her phone rang, just as the person knocked again. She hurried into the kitchen and answered it in a low voice, in case Erma was outside and listening.

"Hello?"

It was Elaine. "Just wanted to let you know that Erma Sherman is standing on your doorstep."

"Is she? You're my guardian angel, Elaine. I was just wondering if Erma might be lurking out there. I've had such a pest-free existence that I knew it was too good to last."

Elaine said, "I know." She paused. "You might wonder how I could detect her there."

Myrtle hadn't wondered this at all because Elaine lived directly across the street and, being in her thirties, had excellent eyesight. But she gathered Elaine wanted her to inquire. "How did you spot her?"

Elaine, thus prompted, happily said, "I have a new hobby!"

"Have you?" Myrtle made a face. Elaine's hobbies were always unmitigated disasters.

"Yes! Birdwatching. I had my binoculars trained on a beautiful male goldfinch outside your house when I saw Erma walking over. You'll be glad to know Erma is retreating."

"Thank heavens," said Myrtle, slumping with relief. "I have far too much to do to endure a visit from Erma."

"Do you? I was worried you might be at loose ends since Miles's family is visiting him. Have you met them yet?"

"I have," said Myrtle. "And they're lovely people. One of the teen boys is *especially* nice."

"Really?"

"That's right. Ben was particularly interested in my sleuthing," said Myrtle.

"Sounds like Miles has been bragging about you," said Elaine in a teasing voice. "It must be nice to be famous."

"Only *locally* famous," said Myrtle, although Elain's words had made her straighten with pride. "But then, it's hard *not* to be locally famous when you live in a town as small as this one."

"Too bad you haven't got a case to work on now. That would have kept you occupied while Miles is visiting with his family."

Myrtle raised her eyebrows in surprise. Apparently, Elaine, despite living in the very same house with Bradley's police chief, was unaware of the mysterious death at Georgia's yard sale. "You didn't hear what happened, then?"

"Something happened?"

So Myrtle filled Elaine in. Which was much more satisfactory than listening to Elaine talk about the different birds she'd seen in Myrtle's yard. Particularly since Myrtle was certain that Elaine would, somehow, mess up even this gentlest of hobbies.

As she spoke, she reflected on how Elaine was the perfect audience. She gasped at the right moments and asked intelligent and thoughtful questions about the event. It was all very satisfying. Once Myrtle had wrapped up her recounting of the incident, Elaine sighed. "Wow. That's just crazy."

"Isn't it? The craziest part is that someone would murder someone else at a yard sale. Right out there in public."

Elaine said, "Maybe they're crazy like a fox. Maybe they thought it would actually prove to be the perfect location because there would be so much activity, it would be tough for the forensics team to get any good information. I wish I knew what the police were thinking, but since Red didn't even fill me in on what happened this morning, that's not the case."

They had a pleasant little chat until Jack suddenly started shrieking.

"Mercy! What's happened to him?"

Elaine sounded weary. "Oh, I think he wants me to pay attention to him. Typical little kid stuff. He's allergic to my phone time. I'll catch up with you later, Myrtle."

And with that, Elaine hung up.

Myrtle worked on her story for the next hour and then emailed it over to Sloan. He should be eager to have every single article she could write for him. The stories were all well-written, with perfect grammar and spelling. They certainly allowed him more time in his day, considering he didn't have to edit them.

Then Myrtle had a very pleasant rest of her day. She finally turned in early. After a bit of tossing and turning, Myrtle wasn't at all sure why she'd thought it was such a good idea. She got up, ate a bowl of cereal, and then tried again after another couple of hours. That attempt met with a bit more success, although she found herself up for the day slightly before four.

It was very annoying, she decided. Ordinarily, she'd pop by Miles's house, fire up his coffee maker, and share her insomnia with her fellow insomniac. But she certainly couldn't intrude while he had family in town, even if they weren't staying with him. It made her feel very virtuous indeed to allow Miles the extra sleep.

But it turned out that Miles wasn't getting extra sleep after all. Which is why, just thirty minutes later, he showed up at her door, already in his usual uniform of khaki pants and a button-down shirt. He gave her a tired smile.

"Gracious! Come on inside. I thought you'd be totally worn out after a murder and a day with your family."

Miles winced. "Perhaps those two things shouldn't be mentioned in the same sentence."

He followed her into the kitchen for coffee. Myrtle peered around at her breakfast offerings. "Cereal? A muffin? Or I could rustle up some eggs."

Miles shook his head and settled at the table with his coffee. "No, thanks. I ate at home, thinking it might help me fall back asleep. But no such luck."

Myrtle was now feeling anxious about her friend. "Is everything going all right? With your visit, I mean?"

Now Miles smiled. "Yes. That part is going pretty well, I think. We all seem to be having a very nice visit. It's just, perhaps, that I'm not all that accustomed to visits. I was so excited that it hasn't been easy to fall asleep."

"It probably doesn't help that you have gotten into a routine of falling asleep late and getting up early. Case in point, yesterday morning."

Miles grimaced. "Don't remind me. Yesterday morning was a mess."

"What are your plans for today? Did you make them before your family left for the hotel last night?" Myrtle tried to sound casual, as if she wasn't really all that interested in the answer.

Miles was apparently onto her, though, and gave her a wry smile. "Trying to see if we have time to investigate before I have activities to attend?"

Myrtle smiled at him.

"Considering how early I'm up, we definitely have time. However, I don't think even murder suspects deserve to be questioned before five in the morning. In fact, those suspects would likely call the cops on us if we showed up at their doors. Red wouldn't be pleased about that."

Myrtle made a face at the thought of how little Red would be pleased about such a pre-dawn phone call. "True. So how much time do we have, say, after eight-thirty?"

Miles raised an eyebrow. "Shouldn't we shoot for nine?"

"Depending on how much time we have."

Miles said, "We've got plans for breakfast at eleven."

"*Breakfast*?"

"Yes. I know that's practically dinnertime for you and me, but it's not an uncommon time for teenagers to eat breakfast. Although I suppose it's technically brunch," said Miles.

"Okay. That should give us enough time to talk to at least one person."

Miles asked, "Who do you think our first early-morning victim should be?"

"I'm thinking Millicent Montgomery, since she was so irked about Victor reselling something from her yard sale. She seems like a likely suspect."

"Do we have a good excuse to go bother her?" asked Miles. "And might she be at church?"

Myrtle blinked at him as if she'd never heard the word *church* before.

Miles continued, "Because it's Sunday morning, after all. People do. I sometimes do, myself."

Myrtle considered this. Then she said slowly, "I don't picture Millicent going to church, no. Although, if she murdered Victor yesterday, she might want to go pray for her immortal soul. Or *immoral* soul, as the case might be."

"There's always that."

Myrtle said, "In terms of an excuse, I was simply going to show up at her house as a reporter. Ask a few questions."

"I'm sure she'll really appreciate that on her Sunday morning," said Miles wryly. "Do you even know this woman at all?"

"I certainly do. She was a former student."

Miles raised his eyebrows. "Oh. A good one?"

"No, a pretty wretched one, actually. And, as I recall, she was the type who never turned in her homework, but kept accusing me of losing it."

Miles said, "She sounds like a joy to teach."

"Yes." Myrtle thought about this. "It occurs to me that I might not have been Millicent's most favorite teacher. Perhaps it would be best if you took the lead in the questioning?"

"*Me*? I don't even know her. What plausible excuse could I have for asking her questions about a murder I think she committed?"

Myrtle narrowed her eyes at him. "I don't think it will be that hard, Miles. I'll show up and explain you're a cub reporter."

Miles said, "No. I'm not the right age to be a cub reporter."

"Fine. I'll show up, say I'm reporting on the incident yesterday, and not explain your presence with me at all. But you'll be sympathetic, as you always are, and Millicent will open right up to you."

Miles didn't look at all sure that was going to happen.

"Just smile a lot," said Myrtle.

Chapter Seven

The two of them killed time for a while in a variety of different ways. There were puzzles to work, more animal shows to watch on TV, and then some time spent dozing off in the chair for Miles.

Finally, they headed off for Millicent's house. Miles fetched the car, Myrtle climbed in, and they headed off.

"There's a surprising amount of traffic this morning," frowned Myrtle.

"Church," reminded Miles, in case Myrtle had once again forgotten.

"This early?"

"There's early service. And Sunday school," said Miles, trying to focus on the road.

Myrtle had forgotten how early it all kicked off. When she'd been a widowed mother with Red in tow, she'd trucked him to Sunday school at ten and then dragged him to the eleven o'clock service. There had certainly been no hope of getting Red out of bed for an early service, if one had even existed.

Fortunately, it looked as if Millicent had no plans for attending church, at least not the earlier service. Her car was still in her driveway.

Myrtle grabbed her notebook and a pen from Miles's center console. "Let's go," she said impatiently.

Miles reluctantly followed her up the walkway to Millicent's front door. It was a very plain ranch house with a neat yard kept even neater by its nearly complete lack of landscaping.

"Rather barren looking yard," muttered Myrtle.

"Shh," said Miles.

"I don't think she can hear me."

But when Myrtle knocked at the door, Millicent was right there, as if she'd been lurking near it all along.

"Miss Myrtle!" said Millicent. "What a surprise."

Myrtle gave the woman a smile. Millicent had an odd sense of style. She wore very colorful tops with equally colorful slacks. Nothing seemed to match. Myrtle was never sure if it was a personal style choice or a severe case of color blindness. "It's very nice to see you, Millicent. Do you know Miles?"

Millicent said, "I don't believe so, no. Good to meet you, Miles. Won't you come inside?"

So they followed Millicent inside. Interestingly enough, the inside of Millicent's home was just as cluttered as the outside was barren. In fact, the number of knick-knacks seemed to give Georgia's house a run for its money. There were also belongings on nearly every surface. Stacks of books, magazines, clothing, and other things.

Miles looked anxious as he always did when he wasn't exactly certain where he should sit down.

Millicent looked vaguely around her. "Let's sit in the kitchen," she finally proposed.

But the kitchen wasn't in any better condition than the living room had been. It all appeared to be clean, but there were dishes, casserole dishes, and plastic containers stacked everywhere. You couldn't see the counter, nor the kitchen table, which was where Millicent appeared to be heading.

"There," she said, gesturing to the kitchen chairs. "Have a seat."

Miles looked even more worried until Millicent grabbed the stacks of belongings off the various chairs and put them on the equally crowded floor.

"Sorry," she said with an offhand shrug. "I'm transitioning from collecting things to selling them online. It's taking a while." Millicent turned to look at Myrtle. "And now, to what do I owe the pleasure of this visit?"

Myrtle went right to the point. "As you might know, I work for the *Bradley Bugle*. I'm writing a story about Victor Fowler's tragic death yesterday. I was hoping you could help me out."

Millicent seemed to relish the idea that she could be in the position to help, or perhaps refuse help. "Oh, I'm not sure if I'm the right person to ask about this."

Myrtle gave Miles a prompting sort of look. Miles sighed. He then gave Millicent a sympathetic smile. "Was it a terrible day for you? I understand you were there at Georgia's."

Millicent seemed to warm up at this approach. "It was awful. Really awful."

"You knew Victor well?" asked Miles.

Millicent appeared to briefly weigh whether it would benefit her to claim any sort of closeness to a murder victim. But apparently, the desire to brag won out. "I did. I knew Victor pretty well." She paused. "He was excellent at the whole resale thing. Victor made a substantial living from buying things on the cheap and reselling them online for a big profit. He knew what types of things would sell well, how to present them online, and what to price them for."

Myrtle glanced around the kitchen. She thought Millicent didn't really have a corresponding grasp of the value of goods. Unless there was an entire market for tacky salt shakers that Myrtle was unaware of.

Miles carefully continued, "And that's the sort of thing you're doing, too?"

"That's right. I'm still trying to learn the ropes, though. I didn't even realize this type of business was a thing until I had a yard sale of my own last year and saw Victor at work."

Myrtle noticed Millicent carefully avoided mentioning any anger over Victor making money off her yard sale.

Millicent continued, "In fact, part of the way I've been learning is by shadowing Victor. I've seen the things he's been interested in at yard sales and flea markets. It's tough to know what's valuable and what's just junk. I tried to go online to figure it out, but there was so much information out there. It was very time-consuming to weed through."

Miles asked, "So Victor invited you to come along as he visited the different yard sales?"

She looked at him blankly. "What?"

"You said you were shadowing Victor," said Miles. "So he invited you to join him?"

"Um, no. No, it wasn't exactly like that. Victor was sort of a lone wolf when it came to assessing items at a sale. I followed him around, but not in any sort of an official capacity."

Miles said, "It must have come as quite a shock when you learned Victor died."

"Well, yes. Of course it was."

Myrtle decided it was time for her to butt in. "Since you were following Victor so closely, I'd have thought you might have seen who the perpetrator was."

Millicent shot her an irritated look. "That didn't happen, though. Red already asked me that."

It annoyed Myrtle that Red had asked this question before she had. "So you weren't following him all that closely? You weren't speaking with him as he walked? Asking him questions?"

"No. Like I said, Victor was a lone wolf. He wasn't the kind of person who wanted me to hang around him. He wasn't nice about it. I mean, he could have acted like a mentor, you know. He'd bait me all the time, taunt me about following him. Jeer at me. Since he wouldn't help me, I just observed what he was looking at. He usually liked to make a quick lap to see everything at a sale, then return during a second lap to pick up the things he'd noticed the first time around. So I paid particular attention to what he was looking at during his sweep."

Myrtle raised her eyebrows. "Then you swooped in and grabbed the items before he came back around."

Millicent scowled at her. "There was nothing wrong with that. I *bought* those things. It wasn't like I stole them. And they didn't belong to Victor."

Miles quickly stepped in again. "Do you have any sense on who might have done something like this to Victor? Was there anyone who was upset with him?"

Millicent snorted. "Oh, he rubbed all kinds of people the wrong way. He could be very abrasive. But I think Jo Fowler is the most obvious suspect. I'm sure the cops think so."

Miles nodded. "Victor's ex-wife."

"Not even *ex*. They were just separated. And I can tell you one thing," said Millicent. She paused, apparently to raise the tension level and the anticipation for what she might say next. "Jo was stalking Victor."

"Stalking him?" chorused Myrtle and Miles.

Millicent nodded, looking smug at giving them the information. "That's right. I mean, I had a *reason* to follow Victor. I was trying to learn his trade. Because I was following him on weekends at the different yard sales, I noticed how often Jo was lurking in the background. She was always monitoring him."

"Why do you think that was the case?" asked Myrtle. "Was she jealous of him and trying to see how much time he might spend with someone else?"

Millicent shrugged. "Maybe. But maybe she was looking for the opportunity to try to get back together with him. Apparently, she really missed him." She made a face. "Which I really can't even fathom. I mean, why would she? He was a cheater. She was living apart from him. It seemed like she didn't have the self-esteem to be by herself in the world."

Millicent glanced at the phone. "And now, if it's okay with you, I've got to get ready to go to church."

"So she was actually going to church," said Miles in the tone of someone who enjoyed having the last word on the matter. They were in Miles's car again, heading away.

Myrtle was barely paying attention. "Didn't you find that whole thing rather odd, Miles?"

"Odd that she's going to church?"

"For heaven's sake, give up on your obsession with church for a second," said Myrtle. "I mean the fact that Millicent was shadowing Victor to figure out how he ran his business."

"Isn't that the way it's been done for hundreds of years? Apprenticeships and shadowing?"

Myrtle said, "Yes, but only officially. From what Millicent told us, she was just following Victor around. He most likely didn't want her there. We've heard from Georgia that Millicent felt Victor took advantage of her by reselling a book that ended up being valuable. He couldn't have been pleased that she was tailing him at all the yard sales. Nor that she was apparently swooping in and scooping up items he showed any sort of interest in."

"Swooping and scooping," said Miles, apparently liking the sound of the phrase. "Maybe Victor was showing *fake* interest. Maybe he'd pretend to find some vinyl records interesting, only to fool Millicent into thinking they might have value."

Myrtle raised her brows. "How very devious of you, Miles."

Miles gave a modest smile. "It's just a possibility." He paused. "By the way, where am I driving? I only have so much time before breakfast with my family. I can't afford to be driving around in circles."

"Let's go back to my house. We still have a little time left. I want to call Georgia."

Miles said, "You think she might have more information?"

"Maybe she has information she doesn't even realize she has. At any rate, I can get a quote or two from her for the next article I'm working on."

A few minutes later, they were back at Myrtle's house. Pasha was sitting serenely on Myrtle's front porch, her tail curled around her feet.

Myrtle reached down and rubbed the black cat, who closed her eyes happily. "What a beautiful girl! Would you like to come inside for a visit?"

Pasha did. Myrtle dug out a can of cat food in the back of her cabinets and poured it out into a red plastic bowl.

"I'd offer you a snack too, Miles, but I suppose it would ruin your appetite for the main event."

"Maybe I should have a very small something. I wouldn't want to appear too ravenous at breakfast. They'll think I don't eat enough, and Dana already suspects I'm hiding health issues from her. Plus, we've been up for a long while today."

Myrtle said, "Nuts? Popcorn?" She stuck her head in the fridge. "A scrap of white cheddar?"

"Nuts, maybe."

Myrtle poured some mixed nuts out onto a couple of plates, and they snacked for a few minutes. Then, of course, they became very thirsty because the nuts were salted. After a couple of glasses of water apiece, Myrtle said, "Now for Georgia."

Pasha, who'd quickly annihilated her cat food, decided to give herself a very thorough bath in the middle of the living room floor as Myrtle retrieved her cell phone.

Georgia picked up the call immediately. "Myrtle? You doin' okay?"

"Just fine here. I thought I might call and see how *you* were doing. And ask a couple of questions, too. I particularly wanted to see if you could provide me with a quote for the paper."

Georgia snorted. "You're in reporter mode, aren't you? Well, I don't blame you. To answer your question, I'm fine and dandy. I didn't sleep much last night, though. I kept getting up and checking to make sure the locks were bolted."

"I'm sure that's a completely normal reaction after having a murder take place in your yard," said Myrtle in what she fondly considered a soothing voice.

"Just to be on the safe side, I slept with my pistol under my pillow," added Georgia.

Myrtle wasn't as sure *that* was completely normal, but she said, "An excellent idea."

Miles, who could apparently hear Georgia's booming voice, widened his eyes.

Georgia was on a roll now. "I've also set up some booby-traps inside the house, just in case somebody makes it inside."

This was decidedly outside the norm. "Are you feeling as if *you* might be targeted, then? You think Victor's was just a random murder? Or that *you* were the intended victim instead of Victor?"

Georgia sighed. "I don't know. The rational part of me thinks Victor had plenty of people who didn't like him. That he was murdered for a reason. It might not have been a very good reason, but a reason, nonetheless. The other, crazier, part of me thinks there's some kind of madman loose in Bradley, and I might be next. Those are the kind of thoughts you dwell on in the middle of the night."

Myrtle thought *madman loose in Bradley* would make quite the eye-catching headline but suspected Sloan wouldn't allow her to get away with it.

"Let's assume Victor was specifically targeted," said Myrtle. "I'm sure that's the direction the police are looking."

Georgia sounded hopeful for a moment. "Do you, Myrtle? You think Red thinks somebody planned on killing Victor?" Then Georgia paused. "Hold on. You don't really know *what* Red thinks most of the time."

"I'll admit that Red, aside from his total obsession with keeping me safe and out of trouble, doesn't often let me in on what's going on in his head. However, I spoke personally to Lieutenant Perkins, and he was all about fibers, DNA, footprints, and things like that. There was absolutely no mention of any sort of madman whatsoever."

Georgia said, "Okay, then! That's great news."

"So maybe you can put that pistol away in a safe, secured location." Myrtle didn't fancy being around a trigger-happy Georgia.

"Maybe so. But not too far away. Now you said you wanted to ask me some questions for the paper? Something like that?"

"Do you have a quote for my story? Something to do with what happened yesterday?" asked Myrtle.

"Yep. Tell your readers that it's tacky to ruin somebody's yard sale by murdering somebody in the middle of it. Oh, and that trespassing is a crime, and I'm fully armed."

Myrtle had the feeling Sloan might also take issue with this particular quotation. But she duly noted it. "Okay. Thanks. Now I wanted to ask you more about your neighborhood and the people in it."

Georgia chuckled. "Won't you get sued if you do? For slander?"

"Hm? Oh, no, this wouldn't be for the newspaper. It's for my investigation. You know how I enjoy figuring things out."

Now Georgia's chuckle became a guffaw. "You mean how you like figuring things out before Red does? Okay, I'm game. First off, Kingston Rowe is somebody you should talk to."

Myrtle jotted down the name. "I remember Kingston."

"Did you teach him?"

Myrtle said, "Fortunately, not. That doubtful pleasure went to the other English teacher at my school. Were Victor and Kingston at odds?"

"You could say that. Victor was on the homeowner association board. He was in charge of architectural review."

Myrtle scribbled down another note. "I assume Kingston wanted to build something on his property?"

"Yeah. I don't remember all the details, but basically Victor didn't let Kingston get what he wanted. Everything went downhill after that. I stopped reading my HOA emails because those two were carping at each other constantly. Then other people would join in, giving their two cents because everybody was on the thread." Georgia snorted. "It sure didn't help keep things harmonious around here."

"No, I bet it didn't. Got it. Well, it sounds like I might just need to pay Kingston a visit."

Georgia said, "You'll bring Miles with you, of course. For protection."

Miles puffed up a bit at the thought of being a bodyguard.

"For *protection*? Is Kingston the type of person who attacks octogenarians?"

"Who knows? People are crazy. Plus, Kingston sure seemed like a hothead in those email threads," said Georgia.

"*Protection* isn't the first word that comes to mind when I think of Miles's skills," said Myrtle. "Besides, he's visiting with his family today."

Miles looked rather deflated now.

"Gotcha. I'd forgotten about that. Want me to come with you?"

Myrtle liked Georgia, but she suspected Georgia wouldn't make half as good of a sidekick as Miles was. Georgia was loud, for one. She also wasn't the type to sit quietly on the sidelines.

"No, I think I should be okay, Georgia. You know I'm able to hold my own. Besides, I carry a cane and I know how to use it. Thank you."

But Georgia had apparently made her own decision. "Nope. Nope. I'm coming along. Wouldn't be able to forgive myself if I didn't come and something happened to you. You were my favorite teacher, you know."

Myrtle stifled a sigh. "If you feel you need to."

"Don't worry, I won't barge into anything else. Just this once. Besides, don't you need a ride?"

Myrtle hadn't considered the driving aspect. Of course, she drove perfectly well—better than most of the horrid drivers in Bradley. But she no longer had a car. She didn't particularly fancy walking that far, either. "I suppose that might work all right," she said, rather ungraciously.

"Perfect. I'll be there in a snap." She hung up.

Miles, having finished his nuts, glanced at his watch. "I should go anyway. Sorry I can't help you out with Kingston, especially since he sounds like he might be a jerk."

"Oh, it's fine. I suppose it will give me new insight into other methods of interviewing suspects. Have a nice breakfast with your family. I guess I'd better get ready, since Georgia said she'd be here in a snap."

Myrtle wasn't quite sure how long a snap was, but Georgia gave a jolly toot of her horn just a few minutes later. Myrtle hoped she wasn't one of those speed demons that went fifty miles an hour on the local roads.

As she walked outside to join her, she saw Erma Sherman from next door, gaping from her living room window.

"Hurry and get in," said Georgia through her open window. "I can't abide that Sherman woman."

"Something we have in common," said Myrtle.

Georgia gave a bellowing laugh. "I knew there had to be somethin'!"

Georgia drove fast enough that Myrtle clutched onto the door to brace herself. Throughout the drive, Georgia provided lively commentary about the people they passed along the way. "You know Buster Donovan? He's painted his house bright purple. Not lavender—purple! Lucky he isn't in an HOA. I feel for his neighbors, though."

A minute later, Georgia pulled up to a two-story house in her neighborhood. It was the kind of house that had a lot going on, visually. There were two stone lions guarding the modest driveway. There were columns on the small front porch. And Kingston's mailbox was painted like an old Volkswagen van.

"Fun, isn't it?" asked Georgia.

"I'm guessing Kingston tried to make his property even more fun, and that's why the HOA shut it down."

"Something like that," said Georgia. "Let's let him explain."

Chapter Eight

The pavers leading up to the front door were big and bold. They were also rather wobbly, so Myrtle was careful to make sure she balanced with her cane as they trod up it. When they reached the front door, Myrtle raised her hand to knock, but Georgia was there first, pounding on the door as if about to perform a police raid. It was a knock that might not predispose Kingston to welcoming the visit.

And indeed, Kingston looked irritated when he arrived, clutching a half-eaten sandwich. He was a tall man with a goatee who looked like he might have played football when he was in high school.

"Wanna talk to you, Kingston," said Georgia briskly.

"Yeah? What's this about?" Kingston looked baffled at the odd combination of the tattooed Georgia and the octogenarian at his door.

Myrtle said, "I'm representing the *Bradley Bugle* this morning, Kingston. I'm Myrtle Clover."

"Oh, I know who you are," said Kingston with a short laugh. "I counted my lucky stars when I didn't get you for English class. I'd have never graduated from high school."

Georgia said impatiently, "Myrtle's writing an article about Victor's death yesterday. Can we come inside?"

Kingston stepped back so they could get past him. His voice was a little querulous. "I don't understand why you want to talk to me about Victor. I wasn't over there at your place, Georgia.

I was here working remote yesterday. My housekeeper can tell you. Bitsy was here, cleaning."

"You can't tell me Bitsy was watching you the whole time. I know that woman is a real worker. So you basically have no alibi?" quizzed Georgia, looking intense.

Kingston glowered at her. "I have Bitsy, as I was saying."

Myrtle cleared her throat. "I'm trying to get some background on Victor Fowler for one of the pieces I'm writing for the newspaper. What you tell me might not go into the story word-for-word, but it'll help me figure out the kind of person Victor was. I'm trying to get some neighbors' views on Victor."

Kingston snorted. "I can tell you the kind of person Victor was. And it's not just my opinion—the neighborhood has reached a consensus on it. He was a real schmuck. He didn't have a lick of imagination. All he wanted was compliance with HOA rules."

As Georgia had mentioned, Kingston looked like he was getting fired up just talking about Victor. He waved his hands around when he talked, forgetting about the sandwich in one of them.

Myrtle said, "I understand there was tension between you and Victor over something you had to pass by the architectural review committee?"

"Tension? Yeah, I guess you could say that. It's not like I was asking to raise chickens in my front yard or paint my house purple or anything. All I wanted was permission to put a flagpole out front. A *flagpole*. It's not exactly something radical."

Myrtle said, "I see. You wanted to display your patriotism."

Georgia gave a resounding laugh. "Tell Myrtle what you wanted to display, Kingston."

Kingston looked at her with irritation. "I wanted to put up my Alabama football flag. It's not that big of a deal, you know. The flag was going to be regular sized. It's not like it was going to be one of those enormous flags that hangs over car dealerships or anything. It was going to be totally discreet."

Georgia laughed again at the idea that a football flag in one's front yard was discreet. Kingston gave her an annoyed look.

Myrtle said, "And apparently Victor stood in the way of you being able to get what you wanted?"

"Right. One of the many problems with Victor is that he didn't think outside the box. I was mad, you know? It's my property. I shouldn't have to listen to somebody else's opinion of what should be on my own land. Anyway, I got so mad about the whole thing that I stopped paying my homeowner association dues."

Myrtle winced. "I have the feeling that didn't go over very well."

Georgia said, "You got that right. Tell her, Kingston."

Kingston sighed. "Victor said the dues had to continue being paid. He levied a huge fine on me and threatened to put a lien on my house. That might have even led to a foreclosure."

Myrtle said, "That's pretty bad. I was curious about the way you said Victor didn't think outside the box."

"He just didn't. He was a pencil-pusher. A rule-follower. I think his role on the HOA board gave him a power trip. He was acting like a dictator."

Georgia chuckled at this. "An HOA dictator."

Kingston shot her another irritated look. "It's true, Georgia. Victor didn't have any imagination at all. All he cared about was crushing everybody's projects. He bullied the other members on the board, too. He wanted to get his way. You should talk to the HOA board about it all, if you want some background. The board was planning a coup to get rid of Victor."

Georgia looked amused again at this. "Political intrigue on the HOA board."

Myrtle made a few notes in her notebook. Then she looked at Kingston. "Do you have any idea who might have done this?"

"Hey, there might have been a dozen people eager to get rid of Victor Fowler. I think you're looking for a needle in a haystack." Then Kingston was quiet for a few moments, as if actually mulling her question over. "There is, of course, one person in particular who might have been especially mad at Victor. Flint Turner."

"Is he married to the woman Victor was having the affair with?" guessed Myrtle.

Kingston grinned at her. "Got it in one. I didn't realize so many people knew about that affair. You're pretty sharp still, aren't you?"

Myrtle gave him a smug look.

Kingston turned to Georgia. "Did you have Mrs. Clover as a teacher?"

"Oh yeah," said Georgia.

Kingston said, "And you *passed*. You must have been pretty good at English."

Georgia shrugged. "I like to read. But the thing was, you didn't really have to be 'pretty good' in English. You just had to get your work done."

Myrtle looked pleased. "That was key. I could fix poor grammar and spelling problems. I just couldn't fix blank pages of homework."

"Laziness! You couldn't fix laziness, you mean," chortled Kingston.

They chatted for a couple more minutes until Myrtle finally stood up. "We should probably head out and leave you to it, Kingston. Thanks for the information."

"My pleasure," he said graciously as he walked them to the door.

Back in Georgia's car, Myrtle said, "You were worried about *Kingston*? He seems completely innocuous."

Georgia shrugged. "I guess he liked you, Myrtle. Believe me, I've seen him act a whole lot scarier than that. Plus, you never know what's going to press his buttons. He could just suddenly go off about something. He's unpredictable. But I'm glad he behaved himself around you. I was going to have to take him out, otherwise."

Myrtle amused herself for a few moments at the thought of Georgia transforming into some sort of superhero.

"Got anybody else you need to talk to? Or am I taking you back home?"

"I think I need to go home for a while. Thanks for toting me around town."

Georgia said, "No problem! I hope you figure out who did this. Like I said before, this one was a little too close to home."

Myrtle frowned as an idea occurred to her. "Red didn't act like you were a suspect, did he? Considering your proximity to the victim, he might have made that erroneous conclusion."

Georgia raised her penciled eyebrows. "That all sounded like a foreign language to me, but I'm thinking you're saying Red might have taken a simple approach to all this and decided I could have killed Victor."

"That's right."

Georgia said, "Well, I believe he considered I might be a suspect. Red seems like the kind of guy who likes to have an easy answer. He asked me a bunch of questions. Did I know Victor? What did I think of him? Did I ever have any problems with Victor? That kind of thing."

"But you didn't have any problems with him," said Myrtle. She knew this because Georgia was an open book. She wasn't the sort to keep secrets. If a thought came into Georgia's head, it was soon coming right back out of her mouth.

"Nope. That's because I never wanted anything done to my house. Now, if he'd wanted to tell me I couldn't have my yard art, then the two of us might have gotten scrappy with each other. Luckily, he never tried that." Georgia looked over at Myrtle. "You're lucky you don't have an HOA in your neighborhood. I reckon you wouldn't get away with your gnome collection."

Myrtle made a face. "Probably not. We have a loose set of rules, though, for the surrounding streets. The trashcans have to be put back out of sight after trash day is over. The grass can't be too long. That sort of thing. But they never say a word to me about anything."

"Ha! Probably too scared. I wouldn't want to be the one to tell you that you couldn't have your gnomes out. You still enjoying that one I got you?"

"I certainly am, Georgia. It's front and center right now for Red's viewing pleasure, as you saw when you picked me up."

Georgia grinned at this. She'd gotten Myrtle a tremendous gnome from one of her yard sales or flea markets. Although Myrtle disagreed with the idea that a gnome could be giant, the apoplectic reaction from Red had been worth any inaccuracies.

A minute later, Georgia pulled up into Myrtle's driveway, gave her a cheery wave and a toot of her horn, and headed away.

Myrtle made herself some lunch and settled down in front of the television with it. She decided not to watch the next taped episode of the soap opera, since it was more fun to watch it when Miles was with her.

She'd just finished eating her pimento cheese sandwich when her phone rang. "Hi there, Sloan," she said. "I've been out gathering information for my next story."

Sloan sighed. "Got it. I suppose I can't get you to work on something else? It's almost time for another helpful hints column."

"I have a helpful hint for you. Don't say another word about me covering the murder."

Sloan sighed again. "Okay. Can I get you to do something else for me, though? I can't seem to get Wanda on the phone, and it's about time for another batch of horoscopes for the paper. Do you think you could track her down? See what's going on?"

"Sure. Maybe Miles will give me a ride later on." Myrtle wasn't entirely sure this was true, considering his family obligations. But, of course, Wanda was family too and Miles had always been rather protective of her.

"You don't think anything's happened to her, do you?" asked Sloan, sounding worried.

Wanda was definitely an asset Sloan would want to protect. She had, by far, the most popular feature in the entire paper. If she weren't writing for the *Bugle* anymore, subscriptions to the paper would drop precipitously.

"Oh, I don't think anything's wrong. If I had to guess, I'd say that Wanda's electricity bill went unpaid, and she doesn't have a way to recharge the phone. That happens sometimes."

Sloan sounded even more agitated at this. "We're going to be coming down to the wire soon. Do you think Miles will get you out there? Otherwise, I could take you there."

Somehow, the thought of Sloan accompanying her to Wanda and Crazy Dan's hubcap-covered shack in the middle of nowhere amused Myrtle. She could only imagine how big his eyes would get.

"I'll let you know later on." Then Myrtle hung up. She still had her potato chips to eat.

She was munching on her chips and watching a very odd talk show when there was a tap on her door. Myrtle put down her plate and hurried off to the door, thinking Miles might be there to give her an update on how things were going with his family.

But instead, it was Wanda, standing on her doorstep. Pasha came bounding up behind her.

"Well, hello! Come in, come in," said Myrtle. "I've been trying to reach out to you."

Wanda came in and settled on the sofa with Pasha. Pasha snuggled up close to Wanda and had her eyes halfway shut as Wanda gently rubbed her.

"Sorry 'bout that," she said. "Phone done died on me. Reckoned Sloan wanted my horoscopes."

Myrtle frowned. "It's broken?"

"Nope. Just overused. Forgot to put it on the charger thing, then got a phone call from Miles. It ran out of juice."

"From *Miles*?" asked Myrtle.

Wanda nodded. "His girl and his grandkids wanted to meet me. Guess I'm some of the only family they got."

Miles did seem to have a very small family. It must be even smaller than Myrtle had thought if Wanda was one of the closer relatives. But she also suspected they were interested in meeting their psychic cousin for other reasons.

"I'm surprised Miles didn't pick you up in his car," said Myrtle, frowning. "That doesn't sound like him."

Wanda shrugged. "He offered, but Dan needed stuff from town, anyway. Miles is gonna take me back home later."

"As much as I'm enjoying our unexpected visit, shouldn't you be at Miles's house?"

Wanda shook her head. "Too early. I'll walk over there in a few minutes. Besides, you got garden club you got to git to."

Wanda was right. In the excitement of the yard sale murder, garden club had somehow become eclipsed. "Won't you come with me? You usually enjoy going. I'm sure Miles could give you a ride back later. Or I could borrow Miles's car and take you back."

"Nope. Gonna be all sorts of shenanigans goin' on there."

Now Myrtle was far more interested in attending garden club than she'd been earlier. "Really? What sort of shenanigans?"

"The sight don't work that way."

Myrtle made a face. "The sight is very particular about how it operates."

Wanda said, "Yep, it is. I jest wanted to drop by and say hi to you. Plus, I gotta give you them horoscopes. I know Sloan is probably tearin' his hair out."

"Well, he doesn't have much left to tear. Let me get on the computer so I can transcribe them."

Myrtle actually vastly preferred the transcription process. She sometimes had to try translating Wanda's written messages, and they were much more difficult. She perched at the computer, and Wanda slowly dictated the horoscopes. She advised Joy Werner not to get on, behind, or under a ladder, told Reece Goodall to get his cough checked out, and warned Milly Pemberton to beware of new friends online.

When they wrapped up, Myrtle said, "Good. Sloan will have one less thing to be worried about."

"Still is gonna be worried 'bout you. And that story of yours."

Myrtle wasn't at all surprised that Wanda was aware of what had happened at the yard sale. She was a psychic, after all. Considering she'd just been advised about the vagaries of the sight, she had the feeling her next question might be futile, but thought she'd ask it. "Any ideas who might have murdered the guy at Georgia's yard sale?"

Wanda gave her a sad look, and Myrtle quickly said, "I know. The sight doesn't work that way. But it was worth a try."

"There is somethin'. I'm tryin' to git it."

Myrtle waited patiently as Wanda tried to pull at the thought that was stuck in her mind. Wanda finally said, "Somethin' about an affair. It ain't real clear."

"Must be that affair Victor was having."

"Mebbe so." But Wanda looked doubtful. "Sorry, but I gotta go." She gave Pasha a last few loving rubs, and Pasha gave her a feline smile. Then, as quickly as she'd appeared, she was gone.

Chapter Nine

Myrtle considered her next steps. She supposed she should speak with Victor's family next. She knew Victor's only in-town family was Dallas Fowler. If she was going to speak with family, it was going to mean she needed to cook. Myrtle always felt cooking should be a creative process, but she wasn't at all sure how creative she could be with what was currently in her kitchen. She'd have to look.

Myrtle prowled about her kitchen for a few minutes to take stock. Pasha watched her with concern. She opened the cabinets and the fridge door. She perused the freezer. Then she made some notes on a notepad.

"I have mac and cheese," said Myrtle slowly.

Pasha looked at her approvingly for the simplicity of the dish.

"But Dallas Fowler is a good-sized man. And mac and cheese is for children. I should add to it to make it more substantial."

Pasha narrowed her eyes at this train of thought.

Myrtle looked in her fridge again. "Okay, I don't have regular milk. But I have vanilla almond milk. That should be fine. It'll add just a delicate touch of sweetness."

Pasha's serious expression seemed to question this statement. Myrtle took note.

"Yes, I know. I *would* go borrow milk, but I don't think it's necessary. Now I just need to figure out the extras. I've got some frozen broccoli and a little ham. That will make it a more satis-fying meal for Dallas."

Pasha gave up and started bathing herself as if she were washing her hands of the entire affair.

"I'll put it together and let it sit in the fridge. Then, when I come back from garden club, I'll pop it in the oven."

Myrtle thought she remembered that the macaroni didn't have to be cooked before being put in the dish . . . that it would just cook when it was in the oven. She wasn't entirely sure how much of the vanilla almond milk to put in, so she followed the package directions and substituted water for the almond milk. Then she chopped the ham and put it in there. After that, she took the frozen broccoli out of the freezer.

"The broccoli will warm up at the same time the mac and cheese is cooking," she told Pasha with confidence.

Pasha looked vastly relieved that Myrtle fed her by simply opening a can.

Finally, with the casserole constructed and left to sit in the fridge, Myrtle ran a brush through her hair and set off for garden club. A newish member was hosting, so she'd had to look up the address and map it online. It was nicely walkable, she decid-ed, and there was no need to ask anyone to pick her up. As she started off down the street, she saw Elaine peering through her binoculars into the trees. Elaine was apparently still birdwatch-ing. It was just a cardinal that seemed to hold her attention. A pretty bird, but very common. At least this hobby seemed in-nocuous enough and wouldn't need to involve Myrtle.

The garden club meeting was in full swing when Myrtle ar-rived. Everyone seemed to be talking about Victor's shocking murder at the yard sale. As she found herself some refreshments, she listened in to see what the buzz was about. But everything she heard sounded like what she already knew. This made Myrtle feel quite smug.

The important thing was to keep away from Erma Sherman, decided Myrtle. She'd gone a fair amount of time without interacting with Erma. Considering the close call she'd had earlier, she had the feeling that her luck might be about to run out. Erma kept looking her way, too, which meant she probably had something she wanted to tell her. It would likely be some really wretched information from her last doctor appointment. So Myrtle kept moving around the newish member's living room, greeting everyone as she made a lap.

Unfortunately, Erma became more determined the more elusive Myrtle became. She finally caught up with Myrtle when she got blocked by a gaggle of old ladies who seemed completely unaware of her need to get around them.

"Myrtle!" chortled Erma. "Gosh, you're slippery today."

Myrtle squared her shoulders, resigned to her fate. "Hi, Erma."

"I had some questions for you," said Erma, grinning at her. "About Miles. I know you always know what's going on with him."

Myrtle gave her a stiff smile in return. "He's currently hosting his family."

"But they're not *staying* with him?"

Myrtle shook her head. "It's a tiny house. You know."

"Couldn't the kids sleep on the floor or whatnot? It wouldn't be much fun in a hotel."

Myrtle disagreed. She thought it would be the perfect setup to host family in a hotel. You get to say goodbye to your family at the end of the day. Your family gets free breakfast and Wi-Fi. They even have a fitness room and a pool to swim in. It sounded like quite a luxurious arrangement. "I think his grandchildren are a little old to sleep comfortably on the floor. Besides, teenagers keep different hours from everyone else."

Erma shrugged. "Okay. Say, I heard you were the one who found Victor. Is that right?"

"I'm afraid I was. Of course, it was most distressing." This was said to keep Erma from being far too excited about a murder victim. She never knew when to stop.

"I bet it was. Of course, nothing could be as distressing as my visit to the doctor yesterday. Do you want to know what he said about my foot?"

Myrtle most assuredly did not. So she took the nuclear option. She fished her phone out of her large purse and opened it up. "Actually, there was something I wanted to share with you, Erma."

Erma looked wary. "Hmm?"

"Yes. I have some really adorable pictures on my phone. I know you love seeing my photos."

Erma started looking for an escape route. "Pictures of Jack?" she asked in a hopeful voice.

"Not this time. I've been scanning pictures on my phone. I've got some pictures of when Red was a little guy that you'll love. Oh, and *here* is one of me when I was an infant. I was a particularly fetching baby, don't you think?" Myrtle thrust the phone at Erma.

Erma looked at the phone as if it had turned into a poisonous snake. "Yes. Very cute. But Myrtle, I just remembered that I need to talk with Tippy about something."

"Really? But I have more photos to share."

"Maybe next time, Myrtle." Erma started moving away.

Myrtle called after her, "How about the next time you show up at my door?"

Erma, looking alarmed, pretended not to hear her.

Myrtle put her phone away, quite pleased with herself. That should prove to be excellent Erma repellant for the near-future. She headed for the snack table to see what the newish hostess had selected for the group. Then Myrtle sighed. It all looked very healthy. There were celery and carrot sticks, fruit, and hummus. She clearly hadn't been to enough garden club meetings to get the memo that fattening and sugary treats were in order.

Tippy, as president, called the group to order. The group, however, didn't seem to want to be called to order. The conversations and some rather loud laughing continued as Tippy frowned.

Myrtle put a few carrot sticks on a napkin and headed for a chair. Tippy smiled at Myrtle approvingly at her obedience. She tried calling everyone to order again, but the lively garden club members continued their raucous laughter.

Finally, Myrtle tired of this. From her chair she bellowed in her best teacher's voice, "Everyone, sit *down*, now!"

Considering many of the gathered were Myrtle's former students, they all froze. Then they slunk to various chairs.

Tippy smiled at them all, although it seemed a bit forced. "Thank you. Today, we're going to have a nice little talk about crepe myrtle trees."

Myrtle winced. She had the terrible feeling that this was exactly why Wanda stated there were going to be shenanigans at garden club. Myrtle was well aware that there were factions at work in their club . . . some pro-pruning and some against it. There was actually a name for this trimming, called "murdering the myrtles," which Myrtle found most despicable. Besides, everyone knew you should simply allow the trees to grow.

Sure enough, as soon as the county extension agent spoke, the garden club ladies were nodding vigorously in agreement with her or folding their arms against their chests and looking bullish.

"But the crepe myrtles will get too big!" protested their Blanche Clark.

The extension officer said calmly, "It's important to have a proper sense of the size of the tree before planting it. They can even end up being thirty feet tall. The nice thing is, though, that they're easy to transplant." This last statement caused the elderly women in the group to stare at her in disbelief.

Erma scowled at the extension officer. "Everybody knows it makes them bloom more."

The extension officer gave her a tight smile. "Only at eye level."

"But everybody does it," said Blanche, staring at the extension officer. "Everybody in town."

"Just because someone else is doing it doesn't mean it's right," said the extension agent as kindly as she should.

"*I* don't do it," said Tippy pointedly. "And my crepe myrtles are lovely."

This was when the room started arguing with each other. Approximately half of those gathered were vehemently opposed to pruning. One woman burst into tears and claimed no one ever listened to her. This led to someone else crying too, in empathy. Myrtle, never a fan of tears, just crunched on her carrot sticks and wondered if they'd ever be able to lure the poor extension agent back to garden club.

The hostess, who was sitting next to Myrtle, leaned over. "Is it always like this?" she asked.

Myrtle shook her head. "No. But this was a very unfortunate topic."

"Yes," murmured the hostess. "I didn't realize."

Things spiraled even farther out of control following that, and several women found this to be the opportunity to complain about other issues that had been on their minds for a long while. Marybeth accused Shannon Weatherby of allowing her dog to use her yard as a restroom. Cynthia Persons said Marybeth bragged too much about her yard when everyone knew her yardman did almost everything in it. Tippy just bit her lip and tried unsuccessfully to corral her unruly garden club group into a semblance of order.

To top it all off, the hostess's clueless husband left the door to the backyard open, and the group was suddenly beset upon by a large dog with uncertain ancestry. Judging from the smell of the animal, who was vastly excited about being part of a gathering, he'd been rummaging in the trash cans. As well, he'd apparently decided to dig in their very muddy yard. The women shrieked as the dog bounded around the room, jumping on some and slobbering on others. The hostess attempted to herd the dog back outside, to no avail.

Myrtle calmly walked into the kitchen, located a bag of potato chips, crumpled the bag in her hands until it made loud crinkling sounds, then tossed a few chips into the backyard. She carefully closed the door behind the dog, who, as expected, immediately followed the chips.

Finally, garden club drew to a close. The extension agent had never regained control of the group, so there was no talk of fertilizing, planting tips, or even when to remove spindly growth. It was all fine with Myrtle. It meant she could slip out of there and head home to put her mac and cheese delight (as she'd come to think of it) into the oven.

She didn't ordinarily call the various people she gave casseroles to before going over. But the fact of the matter was that it was quite a little walk from her home to Dallas Fowler's. It would seem even longer with a glass casserole dish in hand. And, as she had been reminded earlier, it was a Sunday. It was possible that Dallas might be out running errands. Or perhaps he was helping organize Victor's belongings or visiting with a minister to plan a funeral service. Myrtle figured it might be best to call.

But what was his phone number? She fussed to herself at the fact that there wasn't a cell phone directory for the town. She longed for the days of using the white pages of the phone book to look up landline numbers. Maybe, however, Georgia had Dallas's number. It was quite conceivable that there would be a homeowner association directory for all the property owners in that neighborhood.

Georgia did indeed have a phone number for him. She also spent a few minutes talking about what a pain it had been to lug all of her yard sale inside. And she mulled over the idea of participating in a flea market stall that was next to the farmer's market downtown. Myrtle was relieved to get her off the phone, finally. She wasn't often that loquacious, but she apparently had a lot on her mind.

Myrtle tried the phone number, which was apparently Dallas's cell. It went right to voice mail. She sighed. But then, it was good to know if he wasn't there. It put her in a quandary about what to do about her casserole, however. Should she continue cooking it? Or should she pull it out and cook it tomorrow to maximize its appeal when she handed it, warm, to Dallas? Myrtle removed it. With the uncertainty of Dallas being home, she didn't like the idea of putting off the visit until later. That could mean a long walk back home when it was getting dark. It was most annoying to have one's plans in flux. Better to just plan on cooking the casserole tomorrow morning and calling Dallas then.

That decided, the rest of the afternoon and evening was a blissfully quiet one.

Chapter Ten

The next morning, Myrtle woke early and jumped right into action. She got ready for her day, ate a full breakfast, and downed several cups of coffee. It was a cup more than she usually indulged in, and it resulted in her feeling even more energetic than usual. The mac and cheese delight went into the oven, although Myrtle felt it might be too early to call Dallas. She debated morning phone etiquette. Was eight o'clock too early? Eight felt like the middle of the day to Myrtle. Wasn't Dallas likely to go to his job at that point? Maybe seven-thirty would be a good time to call.

Thirty minutes later, she checked on the casserole, poking a knife in the middle to see if it was done. But it didn't seem to be done. She turned up the temperature in the oven and sat back down to do a crossword puzzle.

It was some time later when she started smelling the casserole. Myrtle hurried into the kitchen and pulled the concoction out of the oven. It was well-done on top, which Myrtle preferred to think of as "crisped." At any rate, it certainly seemed to be done.

There was a tap at the door and Myrtle raised her eyebrows. Could it be Miles?

And it was. He smiled at her.

"Miles! You're just in time. I'm about to head to Dallas Fowler's house to speak with him. You can come along and serve as sidekick."

Miles's nose twitched. "Did you cook something?"

Myrtle beamed at him. "Doesn't it smell wonderful?"

"Does it have burned cheese in it?"

Myrtle frowned. "Burned cheese? I don't know what you're talking about. It's a braised mac and cheese and broccoli casserole. I'm calling it mac and cheese delight."

Miles's expression seemed to suggest that he might have come up with a different name for the concoction. "You're bringing it to Dallas?"

"Yes. Are you becoming hard of hearing, Miles? I can certainly speak louder." Myrtle tried out the concept, and Miles shook his head.

"I can hear you." He paused. "I'm guessing you need a ride to Dallas's house."

"Well, that would solve a lot of problems on my end. Georgia drove me to her neighborhood last time when we spoke with Kingston. I was planning on walking, but I was going to have to call Dallas first to make sure it wasn't a wasted trip. Do you have a break from your family?"

Miles nodded. "Everybody is still asleep. Ordinarily, I might be asleep right now too, but my sleep schedule is profoundly broken."

"Then come along," said Myrtle. "The more the merrier. This way I don't have to call ahead. If he's not home, you can just drive me back home and I can try again later."

Miles left to drive his car up in Myrtle's driveway. There was a lightness to her step as she headed for the car. It was good to have her sidekick back. Georgia simply wasn't sidekick material. She was excellent for knocking people off-balance, however. She definitely shook things up. But she tended to take over suspect interviews in a very non-sidekick way.

"Do you have any plans with your family today?"

Miles said, "We're all meeting up for dinner at my house later. But they wanted to make it easy on me, so we're ordering take-out, and they'll bring it with them when they come."

"That's very thoughtful of Dana. She didn't want to put you to any bother."

Miles looked a little anxious. "Will they think it's silly if I set the table? I'd rather eat off a plate and with real forks than out of Styrofoam with plastic cutlery."

"I think it sounds very civilized, Miles. I'm sure they'll think so, too. They weren't raised in a zoo, after all."

"True." Miles paused. "Do you know exactly where we're heading? I've just been driving in the general direction of Georgia's house."

"Goodness! Yes, sorry. I've been thinking about the case." She quickly gave Miles a run-down of where Dallas's house was located, which she'd figured out online.

Miles gave her a quick glance. "What have you found out so far?"

Myrtle was pleased that Miles was interested. No matter how often he seemed squeamish about the actual process of investigating, he was intrigued despite himself. "I had an unusual day yesterday. As you know, Georgia was bound and determined to accompany me to speak with her neighbor, Kingston Rowe. Georgia somehow had the impression that Kingston had a foul temper and might blow up at me. So she came along."

"I've been thinking about that. It's hard to imagine that Georgia thought she might be a calming influence."

"She thought she might be a *threatening* influence. Georgia served as a sort of bodyguard."

"And how was Kingston during the visit?" asked Miles.

"He was agitated when he talked about Victor, but it wasn't as if he was going to shove me out the door or anything. I got the impression at one point that even if it made Kingston angry to talk about what happened, it was good for him to rant a little."

Miles said, "So this was the homeowner association squabble, right? Kingston wanted to build something, and Victor said no?"

"Something like that. It apparently was over a flagpole. I have to admit that Kingston doesn't seem to have the best taste in the world. Victor might have had a point. But the whole thing got ugly when Kingston decided he wouldn't pay his homeowner association dues, and Victor threatened him. His impression of Victor was that he didn't have any vision and that he behaved like a dictator on the HOA board. Kingston said there was even talk about a coup and getting rid of Victor completely."

Miles shook his head. "That's all very messy. Did Kingston have any idea who might have murdered Victor?"

"Oh, he thought Flint Turner might have."

Miles frowned. "I don't know who that is."

"He was married to the woman Victor was having an affair with."

Miles raised his eyebrows. "That definitely sounds like a motive. I'm surprised we're not seeing him first."

"I figured it might be best to talk with Victor's brother before anything else. After all, he likely stands to inherit Victor's property, and I believe Victor did well with his spoils from yard sale reselling," said Myrtle.

"You don't think Victor's wife is in his will?"

Myrtle shrugged. "It depends on how quickly he got around to changing his will after his marriage went sour. He might already have tweaked it."

Miles pulled up to a duplex apartment in Georgia's neighborhood. "Does Dallas live alone?"

"From what I remember, he's divorced and didn't get the best settlement."

Miles parked, and they got out of the car. Miles looked at the casserole on the floor of the passenger side. "Do you need me to carry that?" His expression indicated that he'd rather carry a live snake.

"Hmm? Oh no. I have it in a tote bag for the express purpose of making things easier. I've got it."

Their knock at the door was almost immediately answered by a middle-aged man with Victor's dark hair and slender build. He frowned when he saw Miles, but then smiled when he spotted Myrtle.

"Miss Myrtle!" he said, opening the door to the duplex wide. "Nice to see you."

"Good morning, Dallas. Good to see you, too, but sorry it's under these circumstances. This is my friend, Miles. I wanted to tell you I was thinking of you and to bring by a casserole for your enjoyment." With that, Myrtle removed the mac and cheese delight from the tote bag and thrust it at him.

Dallas happily took it. Miles gave him a sad look.

"Thank you, Miss Myrtle. I'll definitely eat this up tonight. Lemme go stick it in the fridge real quick. Y'all make yourselves at home."

Myrtle and Miles walked into a small living room with threadbare furniture. Everything was neat as a pin, though. Even Miles, who tended to be something of a germaphobe, was good to settle into an armchair.

"Can I get you something to drink?" asked Dallas, reappearing from his small kitchen. "Glass of water? Iced tea? Something stronger?"

Myrtle and Miles shook their heads, and Dallas took a seat across from them.

"We're not keeping you from work, are we?" asked Myrtle.

Dallas shook his head. "I took the day off, considering everything going on."

Myrtle gave him a kind look. "I was just so sorry about your brother, Dallas. What a terrible thing to happen."

Dallas looked somber. "Ain't it? I mean, isn't it?" He chuckled. "Can't be using bad English in front of my old teacher."

"You'd be forgiven, under the circumstances. I remember the two of you in high school together. So awful to lose a sibling."

Dallas nodded. "It's been hard, for sure. I've been thinking back to those old days. Even got my old yearbooks out." He gestured to a rickety bookcase in the corner that held a few books and the yearbooks.

"You were both very athletic, as I recall?" asked Myrtle.

"That's right. Different sports, though, which was probably a good thing. I guess he and I were both pretty competitive. I played baseball and Victor was on swim team and track. We'd help each other train after school. We were a team, you know? Our parents were both hands off, so we supported each other."

Myrtle said, "How nice! And you both ended up living in the same town so you could spend time together and continue helping each other out."

Dallas made a small face. "Well, to a certain degree, I guess we did. But the truth is, Miss M, him and me weren't as close as we'd been in school. Maybe it's harder when you're an adult, and you've got more to juggle. We were both married, both had jobs to manage. That kinda stuff. I had kids, so that didn't make it any easier to carve out time for us to spend together. Now I feel real bad that I didn't make more of an effort to be with him."

Myrtle worked hard not to twitch at all the bad grammar. "You didn't know," said Myrtle. "You figured you had plenty of time left, and why wouldn't you?"

Dallas rubbed his face. "Yeah. But we all know, don't we? We know our days are numbered. That we're supposed to treat every day like it's our last. But then it's just too easy to forget it." He sighed. "That's not the only thing, neither. You'll probably hear it from Red."

Myrtle said, "You know how Red is. He won't disclose anything to me. It's incredibly annoying."

Dallas smiled at her. "I reckon I knew that. Family relationships are tricky, aren't they? Like I was saying, Victor and I kind of hit a rough spot. I had my divorce, and I haven't had two cents to rub together since then. I asked Victor if he could help me out. Spot me some money for my rent."

"And did he?" asked Myrtle.

Dallas shook his head. "Not a red cent. The thing that made me so mad is that Victor *had* it to lend. If he was as broke as I was, I'd have understood. But he had made good money doing that yard sale thing. He told me I'd gotten myself into a jam, and I could get myself out of it."

Miles cleared his throat. "Was the yard sale gig always a moneymaker? Or were there just certain items that made a lot of income?"

Dallas looked as if he'd forgotten he was there. He said, "Well, the impression I got from Victor is that most of the items he bought and resold would make him a small amount of money. Like you're saying, it was certain things, collectibles I guess, that really got him these little windfalls. Then he could afford to make a small amount on the other stuff."

Miles seemed very curious about the entire enterprise. "Was this his full-time job, then?"

"Oh no. It was just a side-hustle for him. I think that's why I was so shocked when he made it big off that one item."

Myrtle said, "We heard it was something Millicent Montgomery sold. Do you know anything about it?"

Dallas snorted. "I know Victor had a good eye for stuff. He went right for things that were worth money. All kinds of collectibles, stuff like that. Millicent had put out a bunch of old books on a table and listed them for a dollar apiece. Victor said most of the books were total trash, but that he saw one right away that was going to be a collector's item. It was a first-edition

James Bond book. And the thing was signed. Victor knew it was going to be a winner."

"I'd imagine Victor made good money off it," said Myrtle. "And I'd also imagine that Millicent Montgomery didn't take too kindly to it."

Dallas's eyes crinkled. "She sure didn't. Gave him an earful, is what Victor told me. She wanted that money back from him. But it wasn't like Victor *stole* the book. He bought it from her, fair and square. He wasn't under any obligation to tell her how much her book was worth. Plus, Millicent didn't even know Victor had a reselling business then."

Myrtle said, "I suppose she found out when the paper ran a story about him."

Dallas nodded. "I told him that was a bad idea. Better not to make people resent you, is what I said. But Victor was right proud of himself. He wanted to let the town know how smart he'd been to recognize the value of the book that Millicent thought was just junk. So there he was, a picture and everything, right on the front page of the paper."

Miles asked, "Did Millicent try to get him to give her some of his earnings?"

"Sure did. Kept coming over and harassing him. But Victor just laughed. He knew he'd got that money fair and square. So then, Millicent decided she was going to start a business just like him. She was about to drive him crazy because she was following him around."

"It didn't seem as if Millicent was as talented at finding valuable items as Victor was."

Dallas shrugged. "Reckon she was just starting out. But yeah. Victor treated it like a real job. He wasn't just visiting yard sales here in Bradley. He was taking road trips every Saturday morning to different towns and different sales. He especially liked them community or neighborhood yard sales where he could knock out a bunch at one time."

"Did Jo accompany him?" asked Myrtle.

Dallas said, "You know they're separated, right?"

Myrtle nodded. "I wasn't sure how long they'd been apart."

"It hasn't been but a few months. And no, Jo thought it was too early on a Saturday. She didn't want to get up before the crack of dawn, get in the car, and drive out of town to see what was usually a bunch of junk. I couldn't blame her." Dallas shook his head. "But it didn't help their marriage much. This side-gig was taking up way too much of Victor's time. His Saturday mornings were full of him acquiring stuff. Then the rest of the weekend was him taking pictures of the stuff, writing up descriptions, and selling it online. It took a lot of time. Then he was back at his office job on Monday. So him and Jo weren't spending much time together, that's for sure."

"Did it seem as if they might get back together again?" asked Myrtle.

"Not to me," said Dallas. "Maybe Jo thought they might, but Victor had already moved on. In every way." He paused. "Red was asking me about Victor's will and whether he'd changed it. Red thought that maybe changing it was just on Victor's to-do list and Jo might've wanted to murder him before he made the change."

"Red's thoughts run in quite dark directions," said Myrtle, raising her eyebrows.

"Well, but look what he's having to deal with. Human nature is pretty awful, ain't it? Anyway, like I told Red, Victor told me he'd changed his will. But he hadn't talked to Jo in weeks. He sure didn't tell her that."

Myrtle said, "So, in Red's mind, Jo had an excellent motive."

Dallas sighed. "In Red's mind, I did, too."

"Has Red been giving you a hard time?"

"Oh, he's just doing his job, Miss M. Don't be telling him off because of that. I reckon he's thinking it's possible I could have done Victor in to get his money. I think Victor left it, or some of it, to me after Jo moved out. I wouldn't have done it though. He was my brother, after all."

Myrtle said, "Have you thought about others who might be suspects? We heard Victor might have had a contretemps with Kingston."

Dallas screwed his face up like he was thinking that through. "If that means he had issues with Kingston, that's the truth. Victor and I weren't so much in touch lately, but I do know that. I guess Victor was trying some sort of power play. He liked to be in control, you know. Plus, Kingston was trying to do something dumb, as usual."

"The flagpole? It sounded rather patriotic," offered Miles, the veteran.

Dallas shook his head. "Shoulda been. Except that the whole reason Kingston wanted a flagpole was to hoist the flag for the college football team he's so crazy about."

"A good alumnus," offered Miles, still trying to be charitable about Kingston.

"Didn't go to college," said Dallas with a shrug. "Just sorta latched onto the team."

Myrtle said, "I've heard Kingston has quite a temper. Do you think he might have had this HOA stuff festering in him for a while until he reached a boiling point?"

Dallas said, "If you mean did Kingston kill Victor, I don't know. He was mad about the flagpole, for sure. Maybe it was of those things where it was the straw that broke the camel's back. You know?"

"I do. It definitely could be a possibility." Myrtle paused and then said delicately, "Since Victor and Jo were taking a break from each other, was Victor by chance seeing anyone else?"

Dallas smiled. "Why, Miss M! You've been listening to local gossip, haven't you!"

"In Bradley, it's very hard not to. Is it true, then?"

"Every word. I saw Anna and Victor together, myself. Guess Victor wasn't trying to hide anything, but I'd have thought Anna might have wanted to. She's still married to Flint Turner, as far as I know. Unless you've heard any differently?" It was definitely a question. Dallas wasn't immune to gossiping himself.

"From what I understand, they're still married," said Myrtle.

Dallas raised his eyebrows. "Well then, I believe I'd add Anna and Flint to the list of suspects."

Miles said, "I can understand why Flint would make the list. Why do you think Anna might?"

Dallas shrugged. "A woman scorned, maybe?" He grinned at Myrtle. "There. That was some fancy talk for you. Maybe a quote?"

"Mm. From William Congreve in the 1600s."

Dallas looked very pleased with himself for conjuring it up.

Miles glanced at his watch with a look of concern, and Myrtle swiftly stood. "Miles and I should head out, for now. Again, we're very sorry about your brother."

Dallas looked more somber now at the reminder. "Well, I do thank you both. I'll enjoy that wonderful casserole, for sure."

Miles flinched at the thought.

Chapter Eleven

A few minutes later, they were back in Miles's car. "I should check in with Dana and see when we're all meeting up again," he said. "She should be up by now. I probably don't have a lot of time."

Myrtle nodded. "That's all good. I think we got just about everything from Dallas that we needed to."

"He seemed like an affable fellow."

Myrtle said, "Yes. He wasn't terrifically upset by his brother's demise. But he was very forthcoming when we were speaking to him. It was good to hear someone else's take on our list of suspects."

"He touched on most of them, didn't he?" asked Miles. "Jo, Kingston, Flint, and even Anna."

"Probably because he was trying to divert attention away from himself as a suspect. Not a bad idea, under the circumstances."

Miles asked, "What did you make of the fact that Victor didn't lend Dallas money when he asked him for it?"

"I think that could probably be Dallas's primary motive for murdering Victor."

Miles widened his eyes. "Even bigger than the prospect of inheriting Victor's fortune? I'd have thought that was the bigger motive, since Dallas needs money so badly."

"It's certainly a *good* motive. I just don't think it's the better motive. I could tell by looking at Dallas how irritated he was over Victor turning him down. Plus, I recall Dallas being a hot-

114

head when he was in school and didn't get his way. He seems much hotter tempered than Kingston does."

They rode along in silence for a few minutes, thinking about their visit. Then Miles said, "What are your plans for the rest of the morning? More investigating? Or are you going to work on another story for Sloan?"

"I want a bit more information for the newspaper article before I write another one."

"Really?" asked Miles. "It seems as if you've collected a pretty decent amount of information."

"Oh, I have. But it's all rather libelous. I need to have different *sorts* of information. No, I think I'll need to find out what's going on with the police side of the investigation now. See what Perkins and Red are thinking. Maybe they had some luck with fibers or footprints or DNA or something." Myrtle sounded somewhat vague on the details.

Miles pulled into Myrtle's driveway. "You think Red will share that with you?"

"It would be over his dead body, if he did. No, I might try Perkins again, although he politely declined to share much last time. But I was wondering if I might get a tidbit or two from my lovely daughter-in-law."

Miles said, "I thought Red didn't really talk about his cases with Elaine. I was under the impression that he realized she might have acted as an informant for you a couple of times in the past."

"That's very true. But Elaine is observant. She might have picked up on something."

Miles glanced into his rearview mirror, frowning. "I'll say she's observant."

"Hmm?"

"She appears to be staring at us through binoculars from her living room window," said Miles slowly.

"Oh, she's looking for birds," said Myrtle in a breezy voice. "It's the new hobby. Birdwatching."

"That doesn't sound as unintentionally dangerous as some of Elaine's other hobbies."

"Right. Nothing much should be able to go wrong with birds. It seems like a fairly innocuous pursuit. All right, have fun with your family. I'll check in with mine."

With that, Myrtle climbed out of Miles's car, walked across the street, and knocked on Elaine's door. It was just a gentle tap because she was well-aware Elaine could see her approach. Besides, it might very well be Jack's naptime and you never wanted to wake up a sleeping preschooler.

Elaine greeted her with a smile and a hushed voice. "Myrtle! Good to see you."

"Naptime for Jack, I presume?"

Elaine nodded. "I have to say I was thrilled. He hasn't had a morning nap for ages, but he seemed to need one today. I have a little more time before it wraps up. Want to have a snack?"

Myrtle wasn't sure that she did. Elaine would suddenly go on health kicks from time to time and stock her fridge with very unusual things.

Perhaps reading her mind, Elaine said, "I have some cheese and crackers. And I could pour you some lemonade to go with it."

This suited Myrtle just fine. She followed Elaine through the house to her very sunny kitchen. Elaine pulled out a hunk of smoked gouda cheese, cut it in pieces, then put it and some multi-grain crackers on a plate and then poured them both some lemonade.

"How's the birdwatching going?" asked Myrtle.

"Pretty good! I seem to see the same birds repeatedly, though. I've lost track of the number of robins I've seen. And the cardinals are plentiful, too. I'd really like to see a bluebird or a goldfinch."

Myrtle said, "You might have better luck watching birds at my house. With my feeders, I'm attracting all sorts of varieties. I'm sure you could catch sight of goldfinches and bluebirds."

Elaine's face brightened. "You think so?"

"Sure. I see them all the time. But they're shy, you know. You'd have to wait them out from inside the house. Or right outside the backdoor."

Elaine considered this. "The only problem is the main time I'm looking for birds is during Jack's naptime."

"You could always let him have a nap at my place. I do have that extra room. Then you could set up shop where you can see the feeders."

Elaine looked pleased. "I might have to take you up on that."

"Do it. I think you'll probably see more birds than you will looking out your living room window."

Elaine nodded. "And don't think I don't appreciate your visit, because I really do. I needed to talk with another adult today, and Red has been slammed, of course. But was there anything in particular you needed?"

Myrtle gave her a smile. "I was just telling Miles how percep-tive you were! And observant, too." Her eyes fell on the binoc-ulars, proving Elaine was even more observant than usual. "I was wondering if you've picked up anything about the investi-gation lately. Any furtive phone conversations between Red and Perkins? Vital evidence discussed? Suspects casually eviscerat-ed?"

Elaine snorted. "As if Red openly discusses the case in my presence anymore. He seems to think I'm your informant."

Myrtle just smiled. "It's not as if I don't use the information for a very good cause. Heavens, the way Red acts, you'd think I was spreading gossip all over town instead of using it to solve his cases for him." She paused. "There was one thing I thought you might help me out with. You're friends with Anna Turner, aren't you? Flint's wife?"

"Oh, I think I know where this is going. And yes, I see Anna from time to time. I wouldn't say we're good friends, but she's in that group of women I sometimes have coffee with after I drop Jack off at preschool. Or sometimes on Sunday afternoons. The group was supposed to meet yesterday, actually."

Myrtle quirked an eyebrow. "And, being so perceptive, as we've mentioned, you might have picked up on some of the rather scurrilous gossip being bandied around?"

"About Anna and Victor Fowler? Yes. I have the feeling it's a bit more than just gossip, I'm afraid. She and Victor used to date in school. Apparently, Flint and Anna's marriage hit a rough spot and she might have taken comfort in Victor's arms."

"Hmm," said Myrtle. "Victor's death must be troubling to her on a variety of levels. She was obviously close to him. And then she'd be treated as a potential suspect by Red."

"Yes! Which is exactly why I asked Red about it. The entire group was worried about our coffee date yesterday. We were all texting each other, trying to figure out what to do."

Myrtle tilted her head to the side. "Because having coffee with a murderer would be a little unnerving?"

"No, more like we weren't sure we could act like our normal selves around Anna. That we'd be awkward, and the whole thing would be a disaster. That's when I told the other women that I'd ask Red if Anna was considered a suspect."

"And was she?" asked Myrtle.

"Not at all. Red relieved my mind on that score. Apparently, Anna had an airtight alibi. She was running errands early Saturday morning, trying to get them done before the shops got busy. There were several store receipts showing her in town during the half hour in question. So we had our coffee together, and a pleasant time was had by all."

Myrtle said, "Even on a non-preschool day?"

Elaine nodded. "It just meant some of us had our kids with us. Jack came along since Red was busy, of course. Jack was very good, actually. The coffeeshop has a blackboard and colored chalk and he loves to color while he's there."

"Of course he does," said Myrtle placidly. "Jack is a perfect angel."

Which was precisely when the perfect angel howled from the back of the house upon awakening from his nap.

Elaine grimaced. "I'm not sure why he wakes up from a lovely nap like that."

"I'll go in there," said Myrtle.

"Are you sure? He's pretty cranky when he wakes up."

"Not with his Nana," said Myrtle in a complacent tone.

Sure enough, as soon as she walked into Jack's room, he sat up in surprise and pushed his wispy red hair out of his eyes at the sight of Myrtle. "Nana!"

"Hi there, my brilliant boy. Did you have a nice nap?"

Jack considered this. Then he gave a small nod.

"If you're like me, and I think you might be, napping is fun until you have to wake up. Then you feel out of sorts."

Jack nodded again.

"Maybe a little bite of something yummy to eat? And I'll read a book to you."

Jack hopped out of his toddler bed at that and grabbed a dogeared copy of *Tom's Truck* which had seen better days. Myrtle was certain she could recite the book from memory, but took it from him, anyway. He slid his small hand into hers and they proceeded to the kitchen for snacks—more cheese and crackers for Myrtle and some animal crackers for Jack. Elaine gave her a grateful look, and Myrtle smiled. She did so enjoy saving the day.

An hour later she was back at her house after reminding Elaine that she could do her birdwatching at Myrtle's anytime. And thanked her lucky stars that Elaine wasn't going to be foisting any unfortunate artwork at her with this particular hobby.

She sat in her living room, thinking about the case. She was glad Anna Turner seemed to be out of the picture for Victor's death. One less person to add to the suspect list. But, of course,

it didn't mean Flint, her husband, hadn't decided to enact revenge on Victor for the affair. Flint might have spotted Victor's
pickup at the yard sale and went to have it out with him. Things
could so easily have spiraled out of control.

Myrtle looked around her small living room smugly. Things
could never spiral out of control there. Except, of course, the
dust bunnies. When she couldn't get Puddin out to clean, the
dust did get rather tempestuous.

She recalled Flint was someone who had come over to do
some odd jobs around the house for her before. The kinds of
jobs that Red was always promising to tackle but never seemed
to find the time for. Red was quite prompt when it came to re-
placing smoke detector batteries or tacking down throw rugs.
But when it came to fiddly things with slow-draining sinks or
clogged gutters, Red was nowhere to be found.

Myrtle decided her gutters could use a good cleaning. In
fact, she couldn't recall the last time they'd been taken care of.
She picked up her phone.

"Flint Turner," came Flint's voice straightaway.

"Flint? It's Myrtle Clover."

"Miss Myrtle? How are you doing today?" asked Flint in his
easy manner.

"Oh, I suppose I'm doing all right. How are things treating
you in the construction industry?" asked Myrtle. She hoped
things weren't treating him particularly well because then he'd
have more free hours for his side-gig of handyman.

"Construction is treating me poorly, Miss Myrtle. Can't
seem to get enough hours to make ends meet. But I've been do-

ing a lot of work on the side. I'm guessing that's why you're calling."

Myrtle was pleased to hear about Flint's employment troubles. "Indeed it is. Red was supposed to clear out my gutters ages ago and hasn't gotten around to it. I'm sure they're filled to the brim with leaves and sticks and perhaps even bird nests. Do you think you could come over and see about them?"

"As a matter of fact, I have an opening in my schedule currently. Would now be a good time for me to slide by? Should only take me an hour."

"Now would be *perfect*. See you soon."

Myrtle hung up. The only bad thing about this particular chore was that Flint would spend the majority of his time on her roof and not in her living room. And she didn't fancy the thought of standing outside and calling questions up to him while he flung debris off her roof. The only way around it was to play up the old lady angle. Fortunately, she was an expert at this.

She pulled out some graham crackers that she kept for Jack and some milk. Myrtle was fully prepared to act lonely and eager for company. Flint, she knew, was quite kind-hearted. Even though he could potentially be a deadly killer when it came to Victor Fowler.

Sure enough, there was a light tap at her door just a few minutes later. Myrtle opened it, smiling. "Aren't you wonderful for coming right over like this! I've been dithering about my gutters for simply ages and you're here in just minutes to solve the problem."

Flint was a nice-looking man with an easy smile, dimples, and dark hair. "Well, that's my job, Miss Myrtle. And I'm happy to do it. I'm sure Red is keeping busy and gutters aren't too high on his list of things to handle right now."

The perfect segue. Myrtle beamed at him. "You're so very right. Victor's death is completely consuming him. Or rather, the investigation of it is. Please, would you come inside and give me a little company for a few minutes? With Red worried about the case and Elaine busy with Jack, I haven't seen anybody for such a long time."

Chapter Twelve

Flint hesitated, rightly wondering how long this visit might last. He apparently came to the conclusion that he could either spare the time or that he could pull away easily enough because he said, "Well, that's right nice of you, Miss Myrtle. I'd love a quick visit before I head up on your roof."

Myrtle gave a tinkling old lady laugh. "I did so hope you'd say that. I pulled out a little snack for us just in case." She gestured to the kitchen and the plate of graham crackers and the container of milk. Flint graciously followed her gesture and headed over to sit down at Myrtle's kitchen table.

"I was thinking about other things that might need to be done around here," said Myrtle. "I don't know if you'll have time to handle them today or not?"

Flint shook his head. "I'm afraid I only have time for the gutters today. But I can come back and handle other things for you. What were you thinking needed to be taken care of?"

"The fence in my backyard needs repairing in a couple of places. Particularly on the side that faces *that* way." Myrtle indicated the direction in which Erma Sherman lived. "That side needs to be very private."

Flint seemed to hide a smile. "Have a tricky neighbor over there?"

"I'll say. It'll be much easier being in the backyard if she can't see I'm there." She paused and waited until Flint had finished chewing up a graham cracker. "I wanted to talk with you a minute about all the goings-on in Bradley."

Flint nodded, looking as if he'd expected a bit of gossip as soon as Myrtle had invited him inside. "It's been a mess, hasn't it? Like we said, Red's staying busy."

"Has he spoken with *you* lately?" asked Myrtle, sweetly concerned. "Of course I'd like to offer apologies for my son if he's been obstreperous in any way."

Flint flushed a little and seemed to study his glass of milk in a particularly focused manner. "Why would Red want to speak with me, Miss Myrtle?"

Myrtle affected a flustered look. "Gracious. I didn't mean to speak out of turn. I may have made a terrible mistake. Or gotten confused. There are so many things going on in Bradley that I might have mixed you up with someone else. I'm so sorry about that."

But Flint seemed both worried and intrigued. "You heard around town that I might have a reason to do away with Victor?"

"Mercy!" said Myrtle, fanning herself. "I shouldn't even have opened my mouth."

Flint was quiet for a moment. "As a matter of fact, I believe what you heard might have been the truth. But I wasn't aware it was public knowledge. I have spoken with Red, but he didn't seem all that convinced that I might be a major suspect." His expression showed that he very much hoped Red wouldn't make a return visit.

"Well, that is a relief. I thought I'd really stuck my foot in my mouth. And don't worry—the whole of Bradley isn't talking right now. There might just be an old biddy or two peddling stories."

Flint asked slowly, "Stories about Anna and Victor?"

"That's what I heard, yes. Of course, I also heard Anna had a lovely alibi, so there is that!"

But Flint still looked glum.

"Did you have a lovely alibi, too?" asked Myrtle.

Flint shook his head. "Not so much. I wasn't at the yard sale, of course. No one could place me there, so that's something. I was making repairs around my house while Anna was out running errands. So I don't have an alibi."

"Mmm," said Myrtle in a noncommittal way.

Flint said, "I hate to say it, but what happened to Victor was karma. You mess people around enough, and you get what's coming to you."

"Did you know Victor well?"

Flint gave a hard laugh. "If I saw Victor coming, I'd cross the street, just on reputation alone. I knew him as well as I wanted to, and that was it. He's been a jerk for years, and I guess I've been conditioned to avoid him as much as possible. If I had a nickel for every time somebody in this town complained about something Victor said or did, I'd be a rich man."

"I'm very sorry about Victor and Anna. What a mess."

Flint sighed. "Yeah. I'm not even sure Anna cares if we stay together. She was talking about us getting separated. She hasn't packed her bags or anything, but the fact that she's talking about it means it's on her mind."

"Oh, I'm sorry."

Flint stared blankly down at his empty plate. "Thanks. I never really saw the sense in separating. If a couple can't deal with each other anymore, they should get divorced. That's what might be in the cards for Anna and me. We're just kicking the can down the road a ways, that's all." He paused. "The thing is, I really still care about her. This all just stinks."

Flint blinked furiously, and Myrtle was suddenly very concerned that he might be about to cry. She swiftly changed the subject. "Thinking back to Victor, do you have any ideas about who might have done such a terrible thing?"

"Red asked me the same thing, so I'll tell you just what I told him. I'm thinking Dallas did it. Victor's brother."

Myrtle dithered a little. "Mercy! A fratricide? How awful."

"Isn't it? Now, remember, I don't *know* what happened, Miss Myrtle, so it's not the kind of thing you should spread around, right? Especially not that it came from me. I don't fancy myself getting beat up by Dallas Fowler for being a loudmouth."

"Of course, of course. My lips shall be sealed. But what makes you suspect Dallas?"

Flint shrugged, "Money. Isn't that always the way? Victor had it and Dallas wanted it. Who'd have thought that Victor's little resale business would make him so much cash? Doesn't seem really fair, honestly. I work my rear end off doing two different jobs and never feel like I've got my head much above water. But Victor waltzes through yard sales, picks up a few bits of people's old junk, and resells it for a mint." He shook his head. "He was a really lucky guy. Until his luck totally ran out."

"And Dallas felt the same way about Victor's yard sale gains?"

Flint said, "I don't know if Dallas thought his brother wasn't working hard enough for the money he was making. All I know is that Dallas was broke. He picked up a few construction jobs with me from time to time when he needed extra cash. Dallas is a hard worker, but never seemed to have two cents to rub together."

"Any idea why Dallas has hit hard times?" asked Myrtle.

Flint shook his head. "When did Dallas *not* have hard times? That family has always struggled, and Dallas lost a lot of money when he had a car accident on his way over to a construction job. He didn't have any insurance at the time and had to pay for his hospital care out of pocket, which just about sank him. He's been dealing with the fallout from that for a long time. Plus, that was followed by Dallas's divorce. That sure didn't help matters."

Myrtle said slowly, "So Dallas asked Victor for money, presumably. And Victor didn't give it to him." She knew this from having spoken to Dallas, but was curious what Flint's take on it all was.

"That's right. Dallas was *furious* with Victor. I mean, I really like Dallas, and I'm not trying to throw him under the bus or anything. But he was furious. I'm thinking it must have really stung that his own brother wouldn't help him out when he was in need like that."

"Mm. I bet it did," said Myrtle.

Flint looked at the rooster clock in Myrtle's kitchen. "Thanks for the snack and milk, Miss Myrtle. You're the best. But I think it's time I get up on your roof and get the junk out of the gutters."

"Thanks so much, Flint. I do appreciate it."

Flint spent the next half hour up on Myrtle's roof, blowing off debris with a blower and throwing other stuff off by hand.

Then he tidied up the yard; a good thing, because Myrtle was sure Dusty wouldn't fancy clearing up the mess someone else had made. Afterwards, Myrtle paid him for the work and he promised he'd be in touch soon about the fence repairs.

When there was a tap at her door just a minute after Flint left, Myrtle assumed he might have left something at her house. So she was surprised when she opened the door and saw Miles standing there with Dana and the two boys.

"Well, goodness! Hello, hello! Have you decided to come by for a visit?" asked Myrtle. "You're in luck. I already have a box of graham crackers out."

"Actually," said Miles, "we're on our way over to Wanda's house."

"Wanda's? But I thought you'd already visited with her."

Dana smiled. "We did. But she was so much fun that we wanted to visit with her again."

Ben, the younger grandson, said, "She invited us to come to her house and give us snacks and everything."

"That sounds like fun," said Myrtle, beaming at the boy.

It actually sounded like quite a startling turn of events. Wanda had never truly hosted Myrtle or Miles in that respect. And, in fact, Miles's concern over messiness and germs kept him from being overly enthusiastic about visiting the hubcap-covered shack that Wanda and her brother lived in.

Miles quickly said, "We offered to bring snacks with us, but Wanda insisted. It sounded like her garden is off to a good start. Anyway, she expressly invited you to come along with us, Myrtle."

"Did she? How delightful! I'll just grab my cane and join you then. Such a nice surprise."

Fortunately, the rental that Dana acquired was actually a minivan. This helped enormously. Myrtle sat in front, Dana drove with her GPS dictating the route, and Miles was in the back being peppered with questions by the grandsons who were the chattiest teens Myrtle had ever come across.

Dana must have read her mind because she looked wryly at Myrtle. "Chatterboxes," she murmured as the boys were giving Miles play by plays on their favorite video games. They'd been rather stunned when he said a chess game was the only thing he played online. Judging from the fervor in their voices, they were determined to convert him.

"It's wonderful," said Myrtle, meaning it. "I can tell you that's not the norm with teen boys. At least, it wasn't the norm when I was teaching."

And then Dana proved how truly charming she was when she said, "Tell me some of your favorite stories from teaching. Dad tells me you've taught just about everyone in town."

It so happened that Myrtle had quite a treasure trove of classroom tales, which had been refined over the years. Dana kept chuckling, and Myrtle kept delivering them. By the time Myrtle had wrapped up, Dana was pulling into the red clay driveway that served as the entrance to Wanda and Crazy Dan's property.

"Wow!" chorused the boys as they saw the house. Myrtle tried to see it as they were, for the first time. There were cars resting on cement blocks everywhere. The yard was broken up by tree roots sticking out of the clay. Sunlight gleamed off the hubcaps that completely covered the shack they lived in. There was a homemade sign that proclaimed the wonders of "Madam Zora," Wanda's stage name. The house and property were quite a spectacle, she supposed.

"This place is so cool!" said one boy.

Miles looked as if he didn't know quite what to say to that. Myrtle interjected, "Yes. It is, isn't it? Let's go knock on the door."

But Wanda had either used the Sight or her sight and knew they were there. She threw open the door, giving them a shy, gap-toothed grin.

Dana gave her a warm hug. "Thanks so much for having us over today. The boys have been talking about nothing else."

Wanda looked pleased but said, "Hope their expectations ain't too high."

"Is Dan here today?" asked Miles with trepidation. Miles was never much of a fan of Dan's tobacco spitting and his erratic behavior.

"Nope. Done gone outta town again."

Myrtle could tell Wanda didn't mind Dan's absence a bit. In fact, she suspected Wanda was likely using the time to clean up. Dan seemed to have an online shopping problem, the evidence of which often piled up inside their small home.

The living room was ordinarily a very dim place. But today, Wanda had the windows open and a gentle breeze was playing through the house. The screens were in remarkably good shape—good enough shape that Myrtle suspected they'd been recently replaced by Wanda herself.

Inside, she'd cleared spots for everyone to sit. This was important because otherwise Miles would be anxious about moving things around. It was also vital because there wasn't a table and chairs anywhere around.

Wanda looked hesitant. "Got some stuff in the kitchen to eat. Mebbe load up yer plates and bring um in here?"

They all headed to the small galley kitchen which, in retrospect, might have been a mistake. The boys were big enough that they could have gotten lodged in there like Pooh in Rabbit's hole. Surprisingly, though, everything went well. No one was stuck. Miles looked very nervous about what Wanda might serve, but seemed relieved when there were raw veggies and dip, nuts, and some cheese. It all seemed very wholesome, reflected Myrtle. The best part was that Wanda might eat like this on her own. There was a healthy glow on Wanda's thin features that ordinarily wasn't present. And, of course, she'd stopped smoking, which was just about the best thing she could have done. Although she still had a worrisome cough from time to time.

"Them carrots is from my yard," said Wanda, nodding proudly at the vegetables.

Everyone murmured admiringly and Wanda beamed.

They settled back in the living room with their plates on their laps. The plates were all from the same set and appeared to be brand new, which could mean they were the result of a Crazy Dan spending spree. Wanda passed out some paper napkins and looked as anxiously at her guests as if she was a mother bird in her nest.

Ethan, the older boy, gave Wanda a friendly look. "How'd you get started with your work, Miss Wanda?"

"Oh, jest Wanda," said Wanda quickly. She considered the question carefully, while Ethan munched on some carrots and vegetable dip. "Well, I reckon it was jest what I wuz born to. Can't do much of nuthin' else. Not smart like you are. You got choices."

Myrtle said sternly, "You are too smart. Smarter than most. You simply didn't have many advantages, that's all. And you're gifted when it comes to the Sight. You need to remember that."

Ben nodded. "Makes sense that you would go into business with something like that. It's a talent not everybody has, you know?" He paused. "You might get a lot more business if you were on social media."

Wanda said, "Sure, I would. But with Dan here spendin' all our money, we can't rightly keep the power on. Can't pay for the internet, neither. Not regular, anyway. Dan gets internet runnin' so he can buy junk online, but we can't never keep it on long. An' it's dial-up, anyway."

Dana frowned. "And all the income is coming from you, Wanda? Or is Dan working?"

"From me. Dan does odd jobs every once n' a while, but not regular."

Dana said, "In that case, perhaps we should set up an auto-draft from the account you both share to a separate, secret account."

Miles and Myrtle looked at each other. They were surprised they hadn't thought of this themselves.

Myrtle said, "Brilliant, Dana. Your father and I have been approaching this from entirely the wrong angle. We've been looking at it from how we can fix the problems Wanda is facing—help pay the electric bill or the gas bill. But you're looking at it from a proactive point of view. Prevent the problem from happening altogether."

Wanda tilted her head to one side. "Ain't Dan gonna wonder why we ain't got no money fer him to blow?"

"I think, for it to work the best, it might be wise to put a *portion* of the money into your secret savings account instead of most of the money from your check. It sounds as if Dan is blowing through the money pretty quickly?"

Wanda nodded.

"Then he's not exactly doing careful accounting of the funds. When he's denied when trying to make an online purchase, or a purchase at a local store, he'll just think he's already spent the money you made."

Wanda nodded again, thinking it through.

"Mebbe could even save up enough to rent a little place somewhere in town," she said slowly.

Myrtle looked delighted. "Is that a goal of yours? That would be *wonderful*."

"Jest would mean leavin' Dan on his own," said Wanda, looking a bit guilty at the thought. "An' leavin' my garden. Not sure I could have a garden if I rented."

Miles cleared his throat. "There's a community garden in town. You get a small plot and can grow what you like there. Of course, you'd have to gauge how much sun the area gets at various points in the day . . ."

As Miles rattled off very scientific-sounding advice on planning a spot in a community garden, Myrtle smiled to herself.

She very much liked the idea of Wanda saving money and getting her own place nearby.

Wanda was nodding carefully at everything Miles was saying. Then she said slowly, "Ain't gonna feel right, though, leavin' Dan on his own."

Myrtle said, "But Dan has the means to make a living, you said? He knows how to do odd jobs. He even did an odd job for *me* once. And don't I recall your mentioning that he used to be a locksmith in a bygone era? I don't think Bradley even *has* a locksmith anymore. The good citizens have to entice locksmiths from out of town to change locks or let them into their houses or cars. It's quite a quandary. I'm certain Dan could make an excellent living back at that trade, if he'd only work."

Wanda brightened at this. "Somethin' to think about."

The boys weren't nearly as interested in Wanda's living arrangements and the dubious ability of Crazy Dan to hold employment as they were about Wanda's psychic abilities. Myrtle and Miles looked at each other. Sometimes Wanda grew both overwhelmed and very weary when asked to provide readings when she was out and about. But Dana insisted on paying handsomely for the privilege and Wanda seemed touched that her young cousins were so interested in something she did. After she'd given them intriguing readings regarding success with books, sports, and love, they chatted happily until Dana gently brought their visit to a close.

As they were heading out the door, Myrtle hung back for a moment. "You wouldn't happen to have any extra tidbits about what's coming down the pipe with this investigation, would you?"

Wanda looked at her sadly. "Gonna be more death."

Myrtle grimly nodded. "I rather thought there might be. And last time, you mentioned an affair. Any extra glimmers on that?"

"Jest a bit. The man yew saw with Georgia."

"Kingston? The one who was angry with Victor for not letting him have a flagpole."

Wanda nodded. "That one. He was havin' an affair with Victor's wife."

Myrtle's eyes opened wide.

Wanda nodded again. "But you need to take care," she added anxiously. "Bad things gonna happen."

"I'm in danger, as per usual," said Myrtle. "Yes. Thank you, Wanda." And Myrtle, who had never been much of a hugger, reached out to give Wanda's bony shoulders a gentle hug.

Chapter Thirteen

The ride back was very lively with the boys talking about Wanda, her "cool house," and their readings. They asked Miles and Myrtle about how her horoscopes worked for the paper and if they could see some. Naturally, both Miles and Myrtle had already had the day's paper out, its puzzles worked, and were happy to talk about the column.

Dana dropped Myrtle back at her house first. She said, "Thanks so much for going with us, Miss Myrtle."

"Oh, it was my pleasure. See you later."

With that, Dana, Miles, and the boys drove away to Bo's Diner. They'd asked Myrtle to come along, but she thought it might be best if they had some time to visit with just the four of them since they couldn't see each other very often. She planned instead on spending the rest of the day quietly at home with Pasha and her crossword puzzle book for company. She even had some time to get a head start on her next article for Sloan.

That night, she slept surprisingly well. So well that she felt quite refreshed at four a.m. Myrtle made herself some coffee, got ready for her day, and collected the newspaper. She did so like it when the newspaper was delivered early.

She was just settling down to a plate of eggs and grits when there was a tap on the door. Myrtle figured it must be Miles, but carefully peered out the window first to make sure. She'd been horrified by an early morning visit from Erma Sherman before and now made sure she was always on her guard. Although she had the feeling Erma might avoid her now that she knew her phone was armed with Red's baby pictures, as well as Myrtle's own.

Sure enough, Miles was standing there, already fully dressed in his usual khaki pants and button-down shirt.

"Come on in and have coffee, eggs, and grits," said Myrtle, opening the door wide.

Miles accepted with alacrity, since those were the only things Myrtle could reliably prepare.

"My mind is just all over the place," he said with a sigh.

Myrtle considered this. "I think you're overstimulated. Think how quiet our lives usually are. And now you've got this rush of activity."

"Our lives are usually consumed with hunting down murderers," said Miles glumly. "Surely that's more overstimulating than a visit with my daughter and grandsons."

"It's just different."

Miles said quickly, "It's not that I'm not having fun."

"Oh, I can tell you are. Seeing you at Wanda's yesterday was a true revelation. You were smiling big smiles. And it wasn't just your mouth smiling—it was your whole face."

"It was nice seeing everything through their eyes, for the first time," said Miles. He paused. "Wanda went to so much trouble for that visit."

"She *loved* it. Every minute. It was worth the straightening up and the food prep to have you all there."

They sat quietly for a moment, sipping their coffee.

"They're leaving today," said Miles in a quiet tone.

"You should visit *them* next. Fly over and spend a week."

Miles looked slightly alarmed at the thought of uprooting his life, hopping on a plane, and spending a week on the other side of the country. "They won't have a free week. They never do."

"But if you're staying with them, they don't *have* to have a free week. That's the fun part of it. You get to see them in their own environment. You can take the boys to school or to their sports. You can watch them play those video games they were talking about."

Miles looked as if he wasn't entirely sure about the video games.

"You can even putter around in the kitchen and make one of those creations you like to make. Dana will love that—coming home to a hot meal for everyone."

Miles said, "I only really know how to make three things well."

"Then you make the three things. The point is that you'll integrate into their lives for a little while. They won't have to entertain you. You'll just be a part of the madness," said Myrtle.

"But then what would I do all day while they're gone?"

Myrtle snorted. "The same things you do here. Work Sudoku and crosswords. Watch pointless television. Read classic literature."

Miles nodded at this. "I see."

"Be sure to tell Dana about it later today. I guarantee you she'll love the idea and those boys will, too."

With that decided, they proceeded to piddle around the house. Myrtle and Miles cleaned up the kitchen and put away the dirty plates. Then they watched a taped episode of their show, which had gotten into a particularly unbelievable realm, even for *Tomorrow's Promise*.

"The writers are really outdoing themselves," mused Myrtle.

"They might be on psychedelic drugs," offered Miles.

After all of that, it was still too early in the day to do anything else. Nothing was open. And Miles's family wasn't even close to being awake yet.

"What's on your agenda for today?" asked Miles.

"Cooking a meal for Jo Fowler."

Miles made a face.

"That's not very nice of you, Miles. Jo deserves a meal, even though she and Victor were separated."

"I'm not exactly certain that Jo *does* deserve a meal, Myrtle."

Myrtle tilted her head to one side. "You're thinking she needs something smaller, perhaps? Having too much food might make her realize how alone she is right now?"

Miles sighed.

"That's very sensitive, I must say. Yes, I suppose if I gift Jo a large casserole, she might feel even more overwhelmed. Hmm. Perhaps I could whip up a smaller dish."

Miles said, "I think the best course of action would be for us to go to the grocery store, pick up a small treat that she might not think of for herself, and then give it to Jo."

"Hmm. Okay. Well then, we should go to the store shortly so I can peruse the selection of ready-made treats."

Miles relaxed into his chair as if a battle had been averted. "Excellent idea."

"So, in the meantime, let's play a game."

"Not Scrabble," said Miles quickly.

"I've accepted the fact that you refuse to play Scrabble with me."

"Nor chess," added Miles.

Myrtle snorted. "Your aversion to playing chess with me does sting, though, I have to admit. I don't even know the names for all the pieces."

"I'm not falling for that again. I'll only play games of chance with you."

Myrtle said, "Well, that rather limits the choices. Two-person games of chance. That sounds like Crazy Eights, Old Maid, or Go Fish to me."

It happened that Miles was quite eager to play all of those games. So they played, won, and lost for the next couple of quiet hours. Then Myrtle looked at her clock.

"It's time for our trip to the store. You'll drive me, won't you? Or do you think your family might be stirring at the hotel?"

Miles said, "I'm quite sure the only person stirring is Dana, and she'll be just puttering around her room. I'll drive you over. Are there other things you need to pick up there?"

"I could stand to get more eggs since we've just gone through a few."

So, a few minutes later, they were on their way to the grocery store. They were passed twice on the way over—once by an ambulance and once by a police car.

"Let's follow them," said Myrtle, looking grim.

"Surely, we're not ambulance chasers now. You're making us sound like the lowest common denominator of lawyer."

Myrtle said, "If the police are heading to this apparent medical emergency, I'm afraid it might be a second victim."

Miles, although still looking resistant, put on his blinker and cautiously followed the emergency vehicles.

"You're going to lose them," said Myrtle impatiently. "Speed up a little."

"That's rich, coming from you," muttered Miles. He carefully and incrementally increased his speed.

Then they saw the ambulance and police car were stopped in front of a small house. Miles parked some distance away.

"I'm not sure we can see what's going on from here," said Myrtle. "We'll have to get out of the car."

"Do you even know who lives here? We also have no evidence whatsoever that this has anything to do with Victor Fowler's murder."

Myrtle shrugged. "The chances it does are pretty high. And no, I don't know who lives here, which is precisely why I want to leave the car to find out."

With that, Myrtle scrambled out, shutting the car door behind her with a slam.

Fortunately, there was a growing crowd of neighbors in various stages of early-morning attire, gazing at the house and talking quietly to themselves. Myrtle walked right up to them, although Miles hung back a little.

Myrtle addressed an older woman first. In her experience, older women were not only quite perceptive, but they were often very nosy as well. "Do you know who lives there?"

The older woman nodded. "She was renting the house and had only been here a short while. Jo Fowler."

Myrtle turned and looked at Miles, raising her eyebrows. Turning back to the woman, she said, "What happened?"

Another neighbor interrupted. "She was murdered."

"Well, we don't *know* that," said the older woman in a severe voice. "You're just making assumptions."

"I'm assuming that whoever killed her husband killed her, too! You know it makes sense."

The two started arguing, which was not helpful. Myrtle broke in with her best schoolteacher voice. "Excuse me! I'm trying to get factual information without speculation. Who called the police and ambulance?"

A small woman who'd been standing toward the back of the group raised her hand, looking rather like an unprepared student.

Myrtle smiled sympathetically at her, trying to settle her nerves. "You did? Did you go over to visit Jo Fowler and find her?"

The woman shook her head. "I didn't really know her. But I knew she lived by herself. And she always seemed friendly. She'd wave every time I saw her."

The man who'd interrupted earlier said, "*I* didn't find her very friendly. She never waved at me."

The older woman sniffed. "That's because you don't wave back. If there's a non-waver, the wavers won't wave."

Myrtle was tired of the diversion into the realm of neighborhood etiquette. She turned back to the small woman. "If you didn't go over to visit, what made you decide to call 911?"

She quietly said, "The front door was wide open. *Wide* open. And it was very early. I get up early to walk my dog, you see, before I go to work. No one is usually up then."

"Why aren't you at work now?" asked the man in a snarky tone.

Miles gave a sigh that indicated he was tiring of the fellow.

The small woman said, "The police asked me to stay to answer questions."

Myrtle, wanting to put a sock in the man's mouth to shut him up, said, "So you saw the front door open during your walk. You didn't worry there was an innocent explanation for that?"

She shook her head. "Not really. But that's because I looked again when Skipper—that's my dog—and I came back from our walk. The door was still wide open. I thought maybe the lady was loading her car or something, but the doors to the car weren't open and I didn't see the lady at all. I called the police and asked them to do a welfare check."

Myrtle nodded thoughtfully. "And then, when they realized who lived there, they brought in reinforcements." She narrowed her eyes as another car pulled up. Looking at the scene in front of him was a horrified Kingston Rowe. She quickly said, "Well, you were good to look out for your neighbors. Um . . . carry on."

With that, Myrtle walked away from the group, with Miles hurrying to keep up.

"What is it?" he asked.

Myrtle nodded to the man in the car. "Kingston Rowe just pulled up."

Chapter Fourteen

Miles said slowly, "The guy who wanted the flagpole?"

"The very one. But not only that, Wanda was able to provide a very helpful bit of information for me."

Miles frowned. "When? Our visit was full of readings and snacks."

"Right before we left. She said Kingston and Jo were having an affair."

Miles's eyes opened wide. "Were they really?"

"Well, according to our local psychic. And Wanda has a pretty good record."

Miles hazarded a look toward Kingston and winced. "He looks absolutely shattered."

"Or else he's an exceptional actor. He could have come here earlier, argued with Jo, had the argument spin out of control, and then killed her. Returning, devastated, to the scene of the crime would provide an excellent cover."

Miles said, "Why would he kill someone he's having a romantic relationship with?"

"Oh, pay attention, Miles! It happens all the time. Maybe he felt stronger love for her than she did for him. Maybe it was the other way around. Or maybe it's nothing to do with the affair at all. Maybe Jo figured out that Kingston, irked at having his beloved flagpole rejected by the HOA board, murdered Victor. Then Kingston had to silence Jo."

Miles hissed at her, "He's coming over. And I'm sure Red will want to question him, so maybe we shouldn't say anything about Jo."

Myrtle snorted. "As if."

Sure enough, Kingston was making his way over to them, on shaky legs. Without any sort of greeting, he said, "What's going on?"

"I'm afraid, from what we've been able to ascertain, Jo Fowler has perished. We're assuming it was a suspicious death, considering what happened to her husband."

Kingston caught his breath raggedly and swerved on his feet. Miles, alarmed, put out a steadying hand. Kingston appeared to take a few deep breaths and nodded at Miles, who cautiously let him go.

"I'm so sorry," said Myrtle. "I didn't realize you and Jo were close."

It was something of a leading statement, but she said it so sympathetically that Kingston didn't seem bothered by it. He nodded. "Yeah. We were friends."

"You were on your way to visit her, I'm guessing?" asked Myrtle, giving him a sad smile.

Kingston suddenly looked more clearheaded. "I was just going to tell Jo I was sorry about Victor. I knew she was still hung up on him, and his death was probably tough for her."

"It wasn't too early for a visit like that?"

Kingston shook his head. "Jo was an early riser. She and I were in an early exercise class sometimes." He looked at Myrtle and Miles. "The two of you are here pretty early, too."

"That's par for the course. Miles and I are fellow insomni-acs."

Kingston looked distracted again. "Red's looking this way."

Myrtle gave Red a little wave, and Red glowered in return.

"He's probably going to give me the third degree," said Kingston, looking a bit panicky.

"Can you give him an alibi?" asked Myrtle. "I'm sure he'd leave you alone with a great alibi."

"Does anybody really have an alibi this time of day? I was just over at my house. I never know when I'm supposed to have an alibi. It's pretty discouraging."

"Maybe Red will be more interested in finding out if you saw anything that could help his investigation," said Myrtle. "You live pretty close to Jo. Maybe he thinks you could have vital information."

"Not if he was looking for information about today. I wasn't around."

Myrtle said, "What about yesterday? Has Jo had any visitors you've noticed?"

Kingston started to shake his head, then stopped. "Well, I did notice Dallas over this way yesterday. It was pretty late. I was kinda curious about that, actually. But that doesn't mean Dallas had anything to do with it. Maybe he was just checking in with Jo, since he was her brother-in-law."

Myrtle said, "Maybe so. That would seem a courteous thing to do."

Kingston glanced over at the onlookers, some of them look-ing his way and talking. He sighed. "People seem to be drawing their own conclusions about me. I guess they've seen my car around here before."

"But they haven't seen you and Jo argue or anything like that? Nothing to suggest you might do her harm?"

"Not a bit," said Kingston quickly. He paused a second. "And I'm not the killing type."

Miles cleared his throat and Kingston, having forgotten he was there, jumped a little. Miles said, "I was wondering about Victor and the state of his marriage. Was it really Victor's affair that caused his separation from Jo?"

Kingston seemed eager to set the record straight. "Jo wanted to keep our affair private, which I understood. Now, it doesn't really matter." He took a shaky breath and continued, "The truth of the matter is that Victor wanted to make everybody think he and Jo separated because of *Victor's* affair instead of Jo's. Because he found it humiliating. That's the kind of guy Victor was. Always had to be the big man."

"Is that also, perhaps, why you didn't get architectural approval for your flagpole?" hazarded Miles.

"Exactly." A red flush rose from Kingston's collar, showing his continuing agitation over the HOA contretemps. "He was trying to get back at me for the affair. Real childish, wasn't it? Truth be told, I felt bad for Jo, stuck in that marriage with Victor. I cheered her on when the two of them separated, even though I knew it was devastating for Jo. Somehow, she still really cared for Victor." He shook his head. "I never understood that. I thought it would be good for Jo to get some distance from Victor. Live her life the way she wanted to. I hated the way Victor talked to Jo."

"He was a cruel man, then?" Myrtle frowned.

Kingston hesitated. "Let's just say he could be very caustic when he wanted to be. And pretty controlling. Jo never said it was anything other than that, but that's bad enough."

Myrtle said, "And now here we are with both of them gone. It's such a terrible tragedy."

Kingston nodded grimly. "If I find out who did this, I'm going after them."

"Last time, you suggested Flint might be behind it. And this morning, you mentioned Dallas," said Myrtle.

Kingston quickly said, "I just saw Dallas around here last night. I'm not saying he had anything to do with any of this. Maybe it was Flint's wife, Anna. Maybe she wanted Victor all to herself and wasn't happy with Jo still tagging around."

Myrtle shook her head. "A good theory, but Anna has a firm alibi."

"Gotcha. Well then, it's probably Flint. The guy seems to have a temper, and Victor had a way of goading people. Maybe Victor was taunting Flint or bragging that Anna would leave Flint for Victor, and then Flint just lost it." He peered through the dark. "Looks like Red is heading this way."

Miles quickly said, "We should leave, Myrtle, shouldn't we?"

"Oh, I think I should at least greet my baby boy first."

Kingston said fervently, "If you want to take over the entire conversation, you're welcome to do that, Miss Myrtle. Or get Red into a better mood. He looks pretty mad right now."

Myrtle suspected Red's anger was likely not directed at Kingston. And indeed, Red came up to her first. "Mama! What are you doing here?" He glanced over at Miles, giving him a reproachful look. "And Miles? I thought your family was in town."

"They're sleeping," said Miles, apologetically.

Myrtle put her hands on her hips. "The only reason we're out is because we were heading to the store to pick up some food for Jo Fowler."

"Really?" asked Red. "Because I'm starting to think you're listening to a police scanner and are tracking me all over town."

"Don't be silly. I have no intention of following you around," said Myrtle with a sniff. "I was simply planning on paying my respects to Jo. An errand that now seems sadly unnecessary, from what I understand."

Red was now focusing his attention on Kingston. "May I ask what you're doing here?"

"I live nearby," said Kingston offhandedly.

Red narrowed his eyes. "Not that close. Were you coming over to see Jo Fowler?"

Kingston looked at Myrtle and then looked back at Red. He seemed to flounder and looked at Myrtle with an appealing gaze, as if asking her to help him out.

Myrtle said, "Kingston was having a relationship with Jo."

Kingston flinched and Myrtle said, "It's better to just bite the bullet and spill the beans. He was going to find out, if he hadn't already." She turned to Red again. "He was devastated when he pulled up. He had no idea what had happened."

"Hmm," said Red in a disbelieving voice. "Is that so?"

Kingston nodded. "It is. I was planning on running by for a visit with Jo. I was at home before that."

"And no one was at home with you to corroborate that, I suppose?"

Kingston said, "No."

"Okay. Mama, Miles, I'd like the two of you to leave the scene now. I need to speak with Kingston in private."

Kingston looked alarmed and Red said, "It's just standard procedure."

Myrtle said, "Red, can you verify that Jo Fowler is indeed dead? And that she was murdered?"

A pulse was throbbing in Red's temple. "Mama, I can't reveal details of the investigation."

"But I'm a member of the press. Besides, if the neighbors know details, it's not as if they're secret. Most of the town probably knows by now."

Red glowered at her. "Just the same, I'm not discussing this with you. And you're *not* a member of the press. You're a helpful hints columnist."

Myrtle seethed. If Red believed those yard gnomes were going anywhere, anytime soon, he had another thought coming.

Myrtle and Miles got into the car and Miles drove them slowly away. Miles sighed. "Red must think we're trying to interfere with his investigation."

"Interfere? We're trying to help. It was mere happenstance that we ended up on Jo's street, anyway."

"I seem to recall following police cars," said Miles.

"Whatever. Regardless, we're trying to help."

Miles said, "Since delivering food to Jo is out now, do you have anything else left on the agenda? It's still pretty early in the day. My grandsons won't be out of bed yet."

"How about breakfast at Bo's Diner?"

Miles made a face. "I've been there a good deal lately. It was where we ordered our takeout last night."

"Yes, but that wasn't breakfast. Breakfast is a completely different experience."

"The *grease* isn't any different," said Miles morosely.

"Then get a bowl of oatmeal. That's what you usually do. I'm feeling too antsy to go back to the house."

Miles said, "You'd mentioned purchasing eggs at the store. Besides, we ate a pretty substantial breakfast earlier."

"Earlier, yes. Quite a *bit* earlier. It's practically lunchtime now. I've burned through all of my energy reserves from that last meal a while back."

So Miles found himself driving back to Bo's Diner so they could avail themselves of the breakfast menu. In the parking lot, Myrtle said, "Puddin is here! I'd recognize her decrepit vehicle anywhere. I've been wanting to get her out to clean for absolute ages. She hasn't been taking my calls."

Miles said, "According to my grandsons, she's been 'ghosting' you."

"Ghosting is an excellent expression and precisely what she's been doing. I'm going to get her to come by my house posthaste."

As it happened, they were walking from the parking lot when Puddin was heading back to her car. She was clutching a greasy white bag of takeout and had a greedy look on her face. Her expression on her pasty-white face changed dramatically into one of resignation when she saw Myrtle and Miles.

"Puddin!" said Myrtle. "I've been trying to get in touch with you."

"Ain't been well," snarled Puddin.

"If you're eating Bo's Diner food, you must have made a sudden recovery. How very fortunate. My house is getting consumed by dust bunnies who are procreating at a frantic rate. You can head over right now if you like. You have the key."

"Don't have it on me, do I?" muttered Puddin, shooting Myrtle a resentful look.

"No, I suppose you wouldn't. That's why it's so handy that I hid a key under one of my gnomes."

Puddin's face was crestfallen.

"It's the gnome that's comically angry over a bee sting. The key is right underneath him. Feel free to eat your breakfast before you start."

Pudding walked away, muttering to herself as she went.

"It's ridiculous what I go through to get help at my house," said Myrtle as they continued walking toward the diner.

"I think it speaks more to the quality of your help. You're dealing with Dusty and Puddin, after all."

Myrtle said, "If I could afford better help, I wouldn't be in this mess." She stopped talking and took a deep, happy breath in as they entered the diner. "It does smell like breakfast in here. No wonder Puddin looked so happy when we saw her."

They were quickly seated and placed their orders. Myrtle got the three-egg breakfast with sausage links, grits, and a side of a single pancake. Miles got a bowl of oatmeal.

Myrtle shook her head. "I don't know how you can be presented with such delicious options and end up with something cold and lumpy."

"Grease, Myrtle. Grease is what is making my decision for me. We don't all have cast-iron stomachs like you do."

Myrtle asked, "Did you have something especially greasy from here last night? When we eat supper here, you always either end up with the house salad or the veggie plate."

Miles sighed. "I was trying to join in. Dana and the boys ordered the tater tot appetizer."

"The one heaped with melted cheese, bacon, and served with ranch dressing?"

"The very one," said Miles. "I guess I lost my mind for a few minutes."

A small smile tugged at Myrtle's lips at the thought of Miles eating cheese tots. "And what did you think of it?"

"It was the best thing I believe I've ever put in my mouth," said Miles honestly. "But I paid the price for it later. The tater tots were chasing me through my dreams last night during the few moments I could actually sleep."

"Those potatoes sound quite athletic." She would have said more about Miles and his sensitive digestive organs, but their food arrived. Usually, Miles looked rather envious of the spread of food in front of Myrtle, but this time, he looked completely contented with his unimaginative bowl of oatmeal.

Miles said, "While I was awake last night, I was thinking about the murder. Mulling things over in my head. I realized I don't think I've been able to cement all the information on suspects and their motives in my head yet. Maybe you could fill me in."

Myrtle was happy to do so in between bites of eggs, pancakes, sausage, and grits. "Well, here's what we have so far. We have Jo Fowler as a suspect. She was Victor's wife, of course. At first, she seemed rather unlikely to have killed Victor, even though spouses are the most likely suspects."

Miles nodded. "Because she was so distraught and clearly wanted to get back together with Victor."

"Precisely. But since that moment at the yard sale, we've learned that Jo was engaged in an affair of her own. She was seeing Kingston Rowe, although Kingston believed Jo was still inexplicably in love with Victor. Kingston, of course, had his own reasons for wanting Victor out of the way."

"The flagpole debacle." Miles stirred his oatmeal.

"Yes. He and Victor had a contentious relationship. And perhaps he was trying to get Victor out of the way. He seemed to really care for Jo when he discovered earlier today that she had been murdered. He stated he didn't like how Victor was treating Jo. Or maybe he was just eliminating his competition. Then we have Millicent Montgomery. She felt wronged by Victor because he sold something she identified as junk for quite a bit of money from all accounts."

Miles said, "So she was just irritated with him for making money off of her?"

"I think it went even deeper than that. She felt wronged. Resentful. Really, almost defrauded by him. Plus, she was going around tailing him so she could figure out how he determined what was valuable and what was worthless."

Miles nodded. "And then you have Victor's brother. Houston."

"Close . . . it's Dallas. He had money woes resulting from a health crisis and a divorce. He asked Victor for help. Victor apparently declined, which may have led to some bad feelings between the brothers. Dallas also believes himself to be inheriting Victor's considerable estate. Considerable to Dallas, at any rate."

The door to the diner opened and Myrtle hissed to Miles, "Look who's coming in now." This left no time for pretense, and Myrtle and Miles gawked at Dallas as he walked through the door.

Chapter Fifteen

He hesitated for a moment when he spotted them, before, to his credit, walking right over.

"Miss Myrtle!"

He smiled over at Miles, and Myrtle quickly introduced him to Dallas as Mr. Bradford. How're the two of you doing?"

Myrtle smiled at him. "Oh, we're doing all right, Dallas. Would you like to sit down and join us?"

Miles winced. He imagined Dallas wanted nothing more than to eat his breakfast in peace, away from a couple of nosy senior citizens. But again, Dallas nodded. "That would be great. I had a brief visit from Red's deputy a few minutes ago, and it's right shook me up. I wouldn't mind working it through my head better."

Miles scooted over and Dallas plopped down next to him. Their waitress quickly descended on the table, batting her eyelashes at Dallas and calling him by name. Dallas was very sweet to her, chatting for a couple of minutes before saying he'd "have his regular order." The waitress sailed off to put it in, ponytail bouncing behind her.

Myrtle said, "I was wondering if you'd heard the terrible news. I'm assuming that's why the deputy was in touch."

Dallas nodded. "Wanted to let me know about Jo, since she was my sister-in-law. Can't believe it. It almost feels like somebody is tracking down and killing the whole family." He paused. "Of course, the deputy also had a few questions for me. Wanted to hear where I was and what I was up to last night and this morning."

Miles asked, "Did the police have an estimate of the time of death?"

Dallas shook his head. "Not a real accurate one. But it seemed like they were a lot more interested in hearing about where I was last night."

Myrtle remembered Kingston mentioning that Dallas had been at Jo's the night before. "I understand you might have visited Jo last night."

Dallas stared at her in amazement. "Look at you! You're just as good of a detective as that son of yours. How'd you find out about that? Never mind—I don't want to know. A good detective never reveals her sources, right?"

Myrtle wasn't sure that was the case, but was happy to keep Kingston's revelation to herself for the time being. "What did they make of your visit with her?"

"They didn't much seem to like it at all. Guess they thought I suddenly became the most likely suspect of all." Dallas made a face. "I was just checking on her, was all. I knew she took Victor's death hard. Plus, I needed to let her know about Victor's funeral service. I'm having it the day after tomorrow. I told the cop that Jo was one hundred percent alive when I left."

Myrtle said, "It sounds like you and Jo had a nice relationship. You were a confidante, perhaps?"

The waitress returned with Dallas's food, her eyes twinkling at him. He winked at her and she chuckled as she walked away. "That's right, Miss M. That's because Victor couldn't be bothered to listen to Jo half the time. That's the kinda guy he was, unfortunately. Even as a kid, he wasn't real empathetic. So Jo would tell me the things—rant, I guess. She felt real bad about the affair. I think she just felt so alone in her marriage that she took up with Kingston."

"Makes sense," said Myrtle.

Dallas said, "Miss M, do you have any idea what Red's thinking about this? I know he tries to protect you and stuff, but I was thinking maybe you'd got some kind of window into his mind."

Miles appeared to be waiting for Myrtle to state, as she always did, that Red's mind was a mystery to her. But this time, she changed her tune, to Miles's growing amazement.

"Well, you know how Red is. But lately, maybe he's grown softer in his old age. He's accepted me as more of a confidante, just like we were saying you were for Jo."

Miles's eyes were enormous.

"He sometimes likes to bounce ideas off me. We've got a tight bond, even though he can be impossible sometimes. Anyway, Red did say something offhand about your financial situation, giving you a great motive to kill Victor."

Dallas heaved a big sigh. "I was afraid of that. And he's not wrong, Miss M. I learned yesterday that Jo was supposed to get everything from Victor's estate. He'd never gotten around to changing that will of his."

Myrtle said, "It was probably just an oversight on Victor's part, Dallas. After all, he'd have had no idea that he was in any danger of dying, not at his age."

"I guess. But it really rubbed me wrong. It reminded me that Victor never looked out for me. He'd even mentioned to me that I was getting everything after he and Jo separated, but he just didn't make the change."

Myrtle said, "And was there a provision in the will for you? In case Jo predeceased you?"

Dallas angrily shook his head. "Nope. The money will go to Jo's family. I know she's got a sister on the other side of the country. The whole thing is such a mess. Plus, I'm a suspect because Red thinks I got the wrong idea about the will and killed two people to inherit." He ate a big bite of pancakes. "Does Red have anything else on his mind, Miss Myrtle?"

Myrtle said apologetically, "I'm afraid he might."

Miles's eyebrows went up at Myrtle's unexpected window into Red's musings.

"He was saying you might have gotten enraged by Victor after asking him for money again. That you're still in a bind, needing money, and maybe you approached Victor at the yard sale to ask him one more time. He turned you down, and you lost control."

"I would *never* have killed Victor, no matter how much he disappointed and failed me. He's family. Our parents are crushed about this, and I'm having to fly them over for their son's funeral. They don't deserve this tragedy in their life, especially at their age."

Myrtle said, "They certainly don't. I hope that justice can be done quickly so they at least feel some sort of resolution to all this. Do you have any further thoughts about who might be behind these deaths? Last time, you did mention Jo, actually."

Dallas sighed again. "I was just speaking off the top of my head, Miss M. I knew how emotional Jo had been lately. I didn't really have any *reason* to think she could have murdered my brother. And now she's gone too. Besides, I also mentioned Kingston, right? It seems to me that Kingston had plenty of reason to want both my brother and Jo gone."

Myrtle said, "You think Kingston had a good motive for murdering Jo?"

Dallas shrugged. "I'm not saying it was a *good* motive, but it sure could have happened that way. Kingston seemed like he cared about Jo. At first, I sorta just thought Kingston was having an affair with Jo just to get revenge on Victor. Maybe that's even how it all started out. But then, I could tell he had feelings for her. Maybe he realized she wasn't feeling the same about him. Maybe the fact that she wanted to get back together with Victor made Kingston upset. Things can get messy when it comes to love."

Dallas looked down at his plate. "Usually, my food would be gone by now."

Miles looked down at his oatmeal, which was in the same situation, and was quickly looking even more unappealing.

Dallas said, "This is all just really hard for me to work through, like I said. You two have helped me out, but now I think we should change the subject to something else. First, let me give you some good news. I've decided that I can't wait around for other people to help me out of the hole I've been in. I'm signing up for some community college classes. I'm meeting with an adviser over there in a few days."

Myrtle beamed at him. "What a great idea!"

"Well, I figure if I've got a skill, then maybe I'll have a more guaranteed income. Can't hurt, anyhow. But that's really enough about me. Tell me how *you're* doing, Miss Myrtle."

And so, for the next five to ten minutes, Myrtle delivered what she considered a very entertaining monologue about her friend Wanda, the hazards of garden club meetings when crepe myrtles were discussed, and how brilliant her grandson was. Dallas made for an excellent audience, laughing at all the right places, encouraging her to say more, asking questions, and generally making Myrtle feel as if she was a most amusing person to be around.

After Dallas finished, he wished them a good day and headed off to the cash register to pay his bill. Then, giving them both a jaunty wave, he headed out the door of the diner.

"That was all very interesting, didn't you think, Miles?"

Miles said, "I thought it was interesting when you said Red liked bouncing ideas off you. I kept peering over to see if your nose would start growing like Pinocchio's."

"Well, it was a necessary means to an end, wasn't it? Besides, he didn't seem to suspect any subterfuge."

Miles said, "No, he was extraordinarily open and pleasant to speak with. Was he always that way?"

"He was. So very unlike his brother, Victor."

Miles said, "I haven't been able to get a really good read on Victor. Different people have said different things, but it's all kind of a mishmash. What did you make of him? Did you know him very well?"

Myrtle shook her head. "Not particularly, no. He was the kind of person who didn't really let others in. Victor was a bit aloof. But I always had the impression he was bright and driven. After all, it takes quite an entrepreneurial person to develop a resale business that's as successful as his was. He was clearly not only dedicated to it, but spent a good deal of time researching to understand what was valuable."

"Which Millicent Montgomery didn't," said Miles.

"Exactly. That aspect bothers me, too. It's as if Millicent was leaching onto Victor's knowledge. It must have irked Victor a good deal. After all, *he's* the one who put so much time and energy into researching and developing his business. Then Millicent thinks she can merely follow him around and cash in? It's a wonder that *Millicent* didn't end up being the victim and Victor a suspect."

Miles finally and unenthusiastically made a couple more stabs at eating his unappealing bowl of oatmeal before shoving it away with a sigh. They paid their bills at the register and then headed back out to Miles's car.

"I certainly hope Puddin is over at the house, cleaning away," said Myrtle.

"I thought it never worked out well when Puddin cleaned while you were out. I'd gotten the impression Puddin only did any real cleaning when you were there in the house, prodding her every step of the way."

Myrtle said, "Oh, I'll likely open my front door and find Puddin watching game shows with the remains of her diner meal all over my coffee table. But I'll soon be able to get her to pitch in. She won't be *happy* about it, but she should be able to be coerced."

Sure enough, after Miles dropped her off, Myrtle opened her door to find Puddin with her feet up, watching a noisy game show with total engagement. She'd clearly long ago polished off her breakfast. Sadly, her breakfast was the only thing she'd polished. Her trash was strewn over the coffee table, as predicted.

"Puddin!" said Myrtle, watching Puddin jump a mile. She'd been so absorbed in her program that she hadn't even noticed Myrtle walking in.

Puddin shot her a resentful look. "Scared me."

"I *should* have scared you. You're supposed to be cleaning my house, not making it even messier. You haven't even started."

Puddin raised her chin and surveyed Myrtle belligerently. "Takin' my break on the front end."

"Good to know. Now your break is over. I have things to do today, and I need you out of my hair," said Myrtle with a sniff. "I don't have time for your foolishness today."

Now Puddin looked curious. "Why're you so busy? Whatcha got goin' on?"

Myrtle said sternly, "There was a breaking news event this morning that I need to cover for the newspaper. I'll need to write the story and get it over to Sloan."

Puddin raised her eyebrows. "You was there, weren't you? At Jo Fowler's house."

Myrtle wasn't a bit surprised that Puddin would know about this. After all, Puddin's cousin Bitsy, who was also a housekeeper, was her constant informant. The only good thing about Puddin was the fact that she often shared helpful gossip with Myrtle. The bad things about Puddin were legion, however, and far outnumbered the good.

"I might have been there," said Myrtle cagily. "What did Bitsy tell you?"

Puddin's pale features looked sulky at Myrtle's assumption that it was Bitsy who told her. "I know plenty of things that Bitsy don't even know."

"Like what happened to Jo Fowler?" asked Myrtle doubtfully.

Puddin pursed her lips. "Maybe not about that, though."

"So, redirecting back to the original point, what did Bitsy tell you?"

Puddin, although irritated that Bitsy was getting all the attention, was still happy that she knew something that Myrtle didn't. She savored that feeling for a few minutes before saying, "Bitsy sometimes cleans for Kingston on a weekend."

Myrtle nodded. It pleased her to know more than Puddin thought she did. "I'd already learned that." Although Kingston's house felt cluttered to Myrtle when she'd been there. He was clearly a man with a lot of pending home projects. And "pending" was the key word. Myrtle wondered how many of those projects actually made it to completion. At any rate, it would have made for a difficult home to clean. Plus, Bitsy was an excellent housekeeper, as opposed to her cousin. And excellent translated to pricy. Bitsy's cleaning services were far outside of Myrtle's budget, to her continuing consternation. Was Kingston really that well-off?

Puddin narrowed her eyes, annoyed that Myrtle had already known that tidbit. "She was cleanin' for him when Victor died. She says he left the house and then came back again in a hurry. Bitsy said there was plenty of time for Kingston to have killed

Victor." Puddin bobbed her head in satisfaction at the interested look on Myrtle's face.

"What was Kingston's demeanor when he came back home?"

Puddin scowled at her. "I done told you about speakin' English."

"How was Kingston acting when Bitsy saw him? What made her think he was at the yard sale with Victor?"

Puddin's scowl deepened. "Because she said so!"

Myrtle put her hand up to her temple, which had started to throb. "Was there anything at all that made her think he'd been there?"

Puddin shrugged. "Said he was acting sneaky when he came back in. An' made a point to talk to Bitsy, so she knew he was back. Now she says maybe he was tryin' to make her be his alibi."

"Hmm." It was food for thought, at any rate. "All right, enough chitchat. Let's get you eliminating those dust bunnies."

For the next twenty minutes, Puddin vacuumed viciously, particularly wherever Myrtle's feet were. Myrtle finally retreated outdoors to escape. She meandered down to the dock, where she had a couple of rocking chairs ready for her. Myrtle plopped down in one of them, stared at the water, and rocked until Puddin came out to demand payment.

Right after lunchtime, Myrtle's doorbell rang. She opened the door to find Dana there, solo.

"Dana!" she beamed. "What a wonderful surprise. No boys? No Miles?"

"The boys wanted ice cream, and I encouraged Dad to take them out. I thought it would be nice for him to spend time with them on his own."

Myrtle wondered if perhaps Dana wanted to spend time with *Myrtle* on her own and maybe ask some questions about her dad. Which she was more than happy to answer.

"Come have a seat," said Myrtle, gesturing over to the sofa. "Can I get you something to drink? Lemonade? Sweet tea?"

Dana shook her head with a smile. "I'm all good. But I'd love to chat with you. Dad talks about you all the time."

Myrtle, who loved being discussed, beamed at her. "Is that so? Oh, and please call me Myrtle."

"Dad is very proud of your crime-fighting acumen, although you scare him to death half the time."

Myrtle swelled with pride. "Crime-fighting. Yes, that's what I do. Although, due to the fact Bradley is such a small hamlet, it definitely doesn't take up much of my time. Not like your full-time job. Or is it full-time *jobs*? Your father was telling me that you're a lawyer *and* a doctor?"

"Well, a full-time doctor. I keep up my law license and practice enough to keep my hand in."

"As one does," said Myrtle.

"But what I do is not nearly as exciting as what you do. Although, from what my dad tells me, it might not be fully appreciated?"

Myrtle said, "Oh, you mean by Red. No, his goal in life is to entrap me at Greener Pastures retirement home. I have to carry out my investigations on the down low."

"In disguise?" asked Dana.

"No," said Myrtle slowly, in the manner of someone who might later try something similar. "But not right in front of Red. And I have to act like a snoopy old lady. Someone who isn't a threat at all."

"Well, however you do it, it works great for you. The stories Dad tells me are fascinating."

Myrtle puffed up a bit more. Then she said, "I must give credit where credit is due. Your father does a marvelous job as a sidekick. I've had other people go along with me when I interview suspects, and they aren't *nearly* as good as Miles. Mostly because the alternates can't keep quiet."

They chatted for a few minutes more before Myrtle said, "And now I'm going to prove that I *am* a snoopy old lady. I've been curious about your mother. But is it painful for you to speak of her? I wouldn't want to cause any hurt."

Dana's eyes lit up. "No, I *love* talking about her. I tell the kids funny stories about her all the time. She'd have loved being a grandma."

Myrtle smiled. "That's nice that you're bringing her to life for your kids." She paused. "Miles doesn't speak of her very often." Miles, actually, didn't speak of her at all.

Dana sighed. "Grief hit him hard. Mom and Dad were very close. They were high school sweethearts."

"That must have been so hard for him when she passed away."

Dana nodded. "Their lives were wrapped around each other in every way. When she got sick, Dad did everything he could to help Mom get well. He didn't want to accept the severity of her diagnosis until it was clear there was nothing else that could be done."

"He's rarely dated here," said Myrtle slowly.

"But he *did* date?" Dana sounded surprised and, actually, rather relieved. As Myrtle suspected, she was looking for a bit of information about her reserved dad.

"Not really. The woman hoodwinked him into it," said Myrtle. "Then she ended up dead, so . . . obviously it didn't go anywhere."

Dana's eyes opened wide. "He didn't mention a word to me about it. Was that one of your murder investigations?"

"That's right. But Miles wasn't truly interested in her. He just couldn't think of a good way to get out of the relationship."

Dana said, "I'm glad he tried, though. Maybe he'll find someone special one day. Special, like Mom was. Here, I have a picture of her." She pulled her phone out of her pocket and scrolled for a few moments. "This is my mom." She said the words proudly.

Myrtle carefully took the phone from her and studied the photo. Maeve looked directly into the camera, as if studiously regarding Myrtle back. Her gray eyes glinted with intelligence and humor. In the picture, she was in late middle-age and wore comfortable, casual clothes.

"She taught school, like you did," said Dana.

Myrtle smiled. "I think she and I would have gotten along well."

"Definitely. She had a great sense of humor and never took life too seriously."

Myrtle snorted. "Then she balanced out your father well."

The two shared a grin. "Yes," said Dana. "Dad tends to be pretty serious a lot of the time."

Myrtle said, "It seems as though they were very close."

"Oh, definitely. Those two gave me this amazing example of what marriage could be." Dana looked rueful for a moment. "Unfortunately, I realized my own marriage didn't come close to measuring up. That's when I knew I needed to leave."

Myrtle nodded. "I rather thought that Miles was a one-woman man. I think, in his way, he's still completely devoted to Maeve."

"They were pretty cute together," said Dana. "He knew she'd grown up camping with her family, so he decided to surprise her with a camping trip. I was away at college at the time."

"Miles went camping? That's mind-boggling. I can't imagine him dealing with dirt, mosquitos, or lack of running water."

"Right? Me either. But it gets funnier than that. Because he wanted to surprise her, he packed the car himself. He found her old tent and threw it in, but he forgot the tent poles."

"That's most unlike Miles. He's ordinarily so very organized," said Myrtle. A smile curled at her lips at the thought of meticulous Miles forgetting something important.

"He's *so* organized. I think he was just all flustered about trying to plan a camping trip when he wasn't actually a camper. Anyway, Mom apparently laughed herself silly when it came time to set up the tent. They managed to improvise with tree branches."

Myrtle's smile grew wider. "A recipe for disaster?"

"Let's just say the tent collapsed on them in the middle of the night and scared them half to death. They decided to sleep out under the stars instead."

"A *much* more appealing solution than using tree limbs in a makeshift shelter." Myrtle leaned in. "Dana, I have to admit that I'm much enjoying seeing a completely different side of Miles."

"More stories?" said Dana, accurately translating Myrtle's statement. "Let's see. There was the time he tried to surprise Mom with breakfast in bed on her birthday."

"The common theme here seems to be that Miles shouldn't surprise anyone," said Myrtle thoughtfully.

"Agreed. Anyway, he ended up burning the pancakes he was making. He set off the smoke alarm. Mom came running into the kitchen, thinking the house was on fire. She laughed a long time at that one, but she was also really touched."

Myrtle made a mental reminder to herself that Miles hadn't always been the competent cook he now seemed to be.

They were sharing stories of Miles's germaphobia, his determination to eat healthy at diners, and his somber picks for book club when there was a tap at Myrtle's door and the subject of their conversation joined them.

He looked at both of their faces and was instantly suspicious. "You've been talking about me?"

"Only in the best possible way," said Dana, giving him a hug. "Are the boys in the car?"

Miles nodded. "Ready to head out?"

"It was nice visiting with you," Dana told Myrtle with a grin.

"Anytime, dear."

Chapter Sixteen

The next day went by quietly. Miles brought his family over so that Myrtle could say goodbye to them before they headed back out of town. Dana paid her a lovely compliment by telling her she hoped she was just like Myrtle when she grew up. Miles's grandsons gave her enthusiastic hugs and said they'd voted her an honorary grandmother.

Myrtle wrote another story for Sloan, this one regarding Jo Fowler's mysterious demise. Elaine did come over for birdwatching with Jack. Jack, less interested in birdwatching than his mother was, played trucks with Myrtle as Elaine botched photograph after photograph of the birds at Myrtle's feeders.

Then the morning of Victor Fowler's funeral arrived. Myrtle, who had a terrible habit of not having her funeral outfits dry cleaned, had carefully scrutinized her choice of garments and found, to her satisfaction, that they appeared to be spot and stain-free. She finished getting ready right before Miles rang her doorbell to drive her to the service.

Miles looked tired but chipper. Far too chipper for a funeral, actually. "Having a good day so far?" asked Myrtle.

Miles nodded. "I am. Of course, it's likely going to be dashed a bit by attending a funeral. But Dana called me last night and formally invited me to their house next time. Like you said, I'll be there in the middle of their usual chaos. But I think it might be a rather pleasant change of pace."

"That's wonderful, Miles! Yes, I think you'll find the comings and goings pretty stimulating. Then, of course, it will also be a relief to come back home to the normal routine."

Miles nodded. "Of murders and funerals."

"Now you're just being silly. We have plenty of other things to offer here in Bradley."

Miles said, "You're the one who's always saying there isn't much to do here."

"There's *plenty* to do here. It's only that I'm an octogenarian, and I've done most of them already . . . quite a few times. Still, the routine can be comforting. And there's always garden club and book club to throw curveballs whenever things get boring."

The funeral was to take place inside one of the local churches and be followed by a reception in the church hall. The family was going to a private burial after the reception. The parking lot had been quite full.

"The church must have lots of different events going on simultaneously," said Myrtle with a shrug.

But when they walked into the sanctuary, they stopped short right inside. There were hardly any spots available, and Myrtle and Miles were there early.

"Mercy!" said Myrtle. They finally squeezed in on a pew near the back of the church.

Miles murmured, "I have to say I didn't expect this at all. Victor appears to have been more popular than I realized."

"I don't think this is evidence of Victor's popularity. I think it's evidence of the size of Victor's family. Look at these people. Many of them have a passing resemblance."

Miles, who didn't have a large family at all, stared at the people making up the full sanctuary. "Amazing."

"Room for one more?" asked a perky voice at the end of the pew. They saw Millicent Montgomery standing there, smiling at them.

Miles was doubtful. "It would make a pretty tight fit." He appeared to want to avoid the prospect of Millicent sitting on his or Myrtle's lap.

But Myrtle was interested in hearing from Millicent. She was on her list of suspects to speak with again, following Jo's death. "Don't be stingy, Miles! I'm sure we can squeeze Millicent in."

But it was indeed a tight fit. Miles said, "Myrtle, there's no room for my arm to be at my side."

"Then put it around me," said Myrtle impatiently. She was still trying to adjust herself on the pew so that Millicent could sit comfortably.

"The whole town will talk," muttered Miles.

"It will be amusing to give them something to talk about. Although I do think this service is mainly filled with out-of-towners."

Then Myrtle turned to Millicent, who'd managed to pry herself into the small spot. "How are you doing, dear?" she asked Millicent.

Millicent said, "Oh, I suppose I'm all right. It's been a hectic week." Her gaze lit across the room where Red was in attendance. He gave Millicent a courteous nod and his mother a weary expression.

"Did Red know Victor personally?" asked Millicent.

"Not really. Just as an acquaintance. But Red usually does try to make it to funeral services for crime victims."

"That's generous of him," said Millicent.

"Oh, I don't think generosity plays into it at all. He's keeping an eye on his suspects," said Myrtle breezily.

Millicent seemed to shrink a little in her tiny spot on the pew.

The organ burst into a bunch of seemingly discordant notes, and Millicent winced. "That's far too loud! And offkey."

This established a pattern that was evident throughout the service. Millicent thought the soloist "horridly tone deaf," the flower arrangements "dreary", Dallas's eulogy "uninspired."

"I do feel terrible about Victor's poor parents, though," Millicent whispered loudly. She wiped some moisture from her eyes. "They've lost their son. Just awful."

Unfortunately, Millicent was one of those people who appeared to have a tough time sitting still. She shifted to pick up her purse from the floor, threatening to unseat the entire pew. She rummaged loudly through the purse during a prayer for a cough drop, which she proceeded to unwrap with an appalling degree of noise.

Miles was in an agony of embarrassment as mourners kept turning to glare behind them at the racket.

Finally, the ordeal was over. No one could stand, though, until the people on the ends of the pew got up and allowed the crammed folks in the middle room to move. And breathe.

Millicent, despite all her rambunctious movement during the course of the service, now seemed perfectly content to stay where she was.

Myrtle had had enough. "Move it," she hissed.

Millicent, flushing, quickly got to her feet, much to the relief of the entire row.

They were exiting the church when Millicent invited herself to stick with Myrtle and Miles for the reception in the church hall. "I don't think I know much of anybody else here," she said with a shrug. "Kind of disappointing."

Miles gave his car a longing look, as if hoping he could magically somehow find himself inside it. Instead, they followed the throng to the church hall, where grouchy church ladies awaited behind tables filled with chafing dishes.

Myrtle was half-hoping that Millicent would lose her mind enough to criticize the offerings the church ladies were serving. She'd end up getting belted with a ladle. It was a very satisfying thought for Myrtle.

Unfortunately, Millicent was on her best behavior. She sweetly asked for chicken and rice casserole, crustless pimento cheese sandwiches, and a couple of buttermilk biscuits before walking off to find a place to sit. Myrtle had her plate loaded with a couple of different casseroles, fried chicken, and loads of ham biscuits. Miles had taken a rather more conservative approach and walked away with green beans, sweet potato casserole, and a fruit salad.

"Do we have to sit next to her?" asked Miles under his breath. "Can't we pretend we've been unexpectedly called to a different table?"

"I believe she'd see through that tactic. Besides, I want to talk to her again. Millicent had plenty of motive to kill Victor.

She was furious with him for reselling something she'd thought was junk. Let's see what she has to say now, after Jo's death."

As it happened, Millicent had plenty to say. "Who would want to kill the whole family? Do the police think Dallas and his parents are next?"

"Oh, I wouldn't think so. That's not usually the case, is it? What I *am* wondering is whether Red has been back around to speak with you again. He does usually speak with suspects a second time, especially if there's been another suspicious death."

Millicent turned bright red. "I'd be appalled that anyone would think I was a suspect. I couldn't hurt a fly."

"But this *isn't* a fly. It's a human being. And human beings can be a good deal more annoying than flies. Did Red ask you where you were when Jo died?"

Millicent muttered, "He did. I was out walking."

"Did anyone see you?" asked Myrtle.

Millicent shrugged. "Not sure. They could have, though. I was out for a while. But when I'm out walking around, I'm in my own little world. I'm not sure I'd have noticed if anyone spotted me out or not. Are you fond of walking?"

Myrtle shrugged. "It doesn't really matter if I'm fond of it or not; I don't have a car."

"Oh, it's so *good* that you're walking everywhere! It's excellent aerobic activity."

And then, completely unprompted, Millicent decided to delve into the extraordinary benefits of walking, the scientific studies she'd read about longevity and walking, the exact amount she walked a day, and how she measured her steps.

Miles gave Myrtle a look that indicated their table assignment was becoming increasingly disagreeable.

Myrtle quickly interrupted the litany of praise to walking. "That's lovely, Millicent. But I'm afraid I'm less interested in talking about exercise than I am about what happened to poor Jo Fowler. It's frightening, isn't it, that there have been two murders in our community in the last week?"

Millicent looked chagrined at the change of subject. Then, apparently deciding she couldn't somehow hijack the conversation and drag it back to the importance of a daily walking routine, she said, "Yes, it's upsetting. I don't know quite what to make of it all. Maybe that's why I'm not very interested in talking about it."

Myrtle ignored the last bit. "You were friends with Jo?" She highly doubted this, since she'd seen Jo and Millicent yelling at each other at Georgia's yard sale. But she was interested in seeing how Millicent handled the question.

"Jo was a dear woman. I had absolutely *nothing* against Jo whatsoever. In fact, I admired her for being in a difficult marriage and handling Victor as long as she did. Victor was always very curt with Jo every time I saw them out together."

Miles cleared his throat. "Did you feel Jo was also to blame for profiting off the resale of your property?"

Millicent gave him a disappointed look as if a teddy bear had suddenly transformed itself into a grizzly. "My beef was *never* with Jo. I feel simply awful that she's gone. She was a great woman." She paused. "Of course, I always felt sorry for her and her terrible sense of style. Plus, she was an absolutely wretched housekeeper."

"You've been in Victor and Jo's house, then?" asked Myrtle smoothly.

"Only once. It was after my yard sale and not long after I realized I'd been had. I walked over there to reason with Victor. I wanted to make sure he knew that he'd basically stolen a nest egg from me and made me look like a fool on top of it all. Victor just sat and sneered at me, but Jo was lovely and brought me a coffee and some cookies. The cookies weren't very tasty, as I recall, but they were palatable."

Myrtle said, "The last time I spoke with you, you'd thought Jo had probably killed Victor."

Millicent gave an awkward laugh. "Well, sure. I thought she *must* have, considering how impossible Victor was. Why wouldn't she? He was truly awful to her. And then he was off gallivanting with another woman. A *married* woman." Millicent shook her head.

"But why would Jo have wanted to kill Victor when they were already separated from each other and appeared to be going their separate ways?" asked Myrtle.

Millicent heaved an impatient sigh. "How should I know? Maybe Jo wanted a divorce, and Victor didn't want to give her one. Or it could have been the other way around, and *Victor* wanted a divorce, which hurt Jo's feelings. Or maybe Victor said he was going to take Jo to divorce court, air all their dirty laundry, and not give her a dime in the proceedings." She paused. "Actually, that last one makes sense. In this town, the airing of dirty laundry would be a nightmare. They even seem to be talking about *me* here."

"Are they?" asked Myrtle.

"They have too much time on their hands in Bradley. Nothing to do but talk. I certainly didn't kill anyone, but you'd think I was some sort of serial killer the way people look at me. Yes, I argued with Victor. But, once I realized I wasn't going to get anywhere with him, I decided to try a different tactic. He wasn't going to give any money to me that he made from selling my James Bond book. But he could help me out in other ways. That's why I was tailing him, of course."

Miles said thoughtfully, "So it wasn't that you were just trying to grab anything potentially valuable before Victor could."

Millicent snorted. "Well, maybe that was part of it, too. Victor always made a lap around a yard sale before he'd commit to anything. But I was mostly trying to learn what he was doing. Now I'm going to expand on what I've learned from him. I'm going to take my new skills farther afield and try them out in another town this weekend."

"That sounds like a good thing to do," said Myrtle. "Move forward."

"Maybe I'll even find a first edition James Bond book," said Millicent lightly.

Millicent then started chatting with great determination about collectible books. She was interested in hearing what sorts of books Miles and Myrtle thought might be valuable and then correcting them or agreeing with them. She'd ended up doing more research on antiquarian and rare books after her debacle. Then, finally spotting an acquaintance of hers at the funeral reception, she rose, said goodbye, and left.

Miles looked vastly relieved. "She's very stressful to be around."

"Is she? I thought her merely annoying," said Myrtle.

"It's all that compressed energy plus the accelerant of constant snide comments. It's exhausting. And intense."

"Mmm," said Myrtle. "You're right. She pointed out the shortcomings of the service all the way through. Almost as if it were a performance she'd paid to see instead of a funeral service."

"Whatever it was, it's nice to have it stop." They both sat quietly, drinking sweet tea and looking around the room. Red was still there and gave a small eye-roll when Myrtle glanced his way. As usual, he thought she was snooping, she supposed. Which, of course, made her peer in the direction he'd been looking in before his eye-roll. She saw Flint Turner, eating a fried chicken plate and chatting with people at his table.

"Flint Turner is here," said Myrtle. "That's rather surprising. He certainly wasn't a fan of Victor's. Not considering his wife was having an affair with him."

Miles said, "Maybe he thought he should let bygones be bygones."

"Hm. Far more likely that he thought it would look bad if he didn't come. I'll have to call him up and have him come out to the house again. He's supposed to look at my fence."

"The fence on Erma's side?" Miles raised an eyebrow. "You'll want that shored up, for sure."

"Precisely. It was a chore I've been meaning to hire out for a while. It's particularly convenient timing now, when I'm wanting to speak with Flint."

Miles said, "You don't want to speak with him now?"

"Not with Red glowering at me. It's better if Flint just comes over later. Maybe even this afternoon. I don't see why he couldn't. And now, I think we should go. As far as I can tell, I haven't spilled anything on my funeral clothes, and I want to leave while that's still true. After all, we'll have Jo Fowler's service to attend in the near future." They left the building and started walking for Miles's car. "I wonder if I should cook something for Kingston," mulled Myrtle. He did seem very upset over poor Jo's demise."

Miles hastily said, "Kingston is fine, I'm sure."

Something in his tone rankled Myrtle a bit. "Is he? Are you sure you wouldn't want to burn some pancakes for him? Perhaps setting off the smoke detector in the process?"

Miles stared at her, face flushing. Then his brows drew together. "You've been talking to Dana."

"Which was so much fun! I ended up with a completely different perspective on you."

Miles muttered, "An outdated one. After that incident, I made certain to perfect my kitchen skills. And always use a timer."

"I think it's just sweet how you kept trying to surprise Maeve, with less-than-perfect results. It shows resilience."

Miles seemed eager to change the subject. "Thanks. I guess. Thinking again on Jo's upcoming service, isn't it a pity that so much of our social life seems to revolve around funerals?"

Myrtle shrugged. "Funerals are often better than weddings. Weddings can get mawkish. The food is much better at funerals, too."

Miles demurred. "No, I disagree with you there. Wedding food is usually excellent." They climbed into his car and he drove away from the church.

"A matter of taste, perhaps. Wedding food is always fairly healthy. Plus, you don't feel right loading up your plate at a wedding unless it's a very lavish affair. The bride's father always tends to look pitifully anxious over the cost of the event. At a funeral, there are heaps of food. It's all very heavy Southern cooking, too, by women whose skills are aged to perfection. Plus, everyone is usually in good spirits at a funeral."

Miles lifted an eyebrow. "I'd love to hear you elaborate on that statement."

"It's very true, Miles. Everyone at a funeral has been put through an emotional, sorrowful service. They're eager for the cathartic experience of a reception to cheer everyone up. Even Victor's parents looked more upbeat than they did at the funeral."

"Weddings often serve alcohol. Funerals often don't," observed Miles.

"Moot point, since you and I drink very little. Plus, we've both been at weddings where guests were over-served. It made for a very dreary experience for everyone but the revelers themselves."

They were still engaged in lively discussion of the merits of funerals over weddings and weddings over funerals until Miles pulled the car into Myrtle's driveway. "Anyway," said Myrtle as she got out of the car, "there happen to be many more funerals in Bradley than there are weddings."

Satisfied with her parting shot, she walked to the door.

Chapter Seventeen

After carefully hanging up her funeral outfit and ensuring that it was indeed stain-free, Myrtle decided to work a crossword puzzle and wait until Flint was likely back home from the service. While she worked on her puzzle, she heard a scratching at the front window. Pasha was staring in at her with a feline smile on her face.

"What a brilliant, lovely girl you are!" crooned Myrtle as she let the black cat into her house.

Pasha blinked slowly at her, eyes gleaming.

"Would you like a little snack? I did remember to pick up cat food at the store. I think Elaine would like it if I ensured you were well-fed. She's watching the birds, you know."

Pasha's expression indicated that she was watching birds herself. Myrtle fixed her a can of food and Pasha happily consumed it before grooming herself.

There was a tap at Myrtle's door. She opened it to find Flint Turner there. "The very man I was thinking of!" said Myrtle, ushering him in. "I was going to call you this afternoon. How fortuitous that you showed up."

Flint was no longer wearing the suit he had on at the service. Instead, he wore his work clothes. "Well," he said, "I spotted you as you and Miles were leaving Victor's funeral. I couldn't catch you before you left to ask if it was an okay time. Is it?"

"The most perfect of times. I saw you at the reception, but you appeared to be engaged in conversation at the time. I was actually a bit surprised to see you there."

Flint nodded. "I'm sure you were, considering. I figured it would be good for the optics. Especially since Red was there. I didn't want Red to think I was hiding or anything." He sighed. "Red talked to me again yesterday. I feel like I'm really on his radar."

"Everyone is on his radar right now. The police are probably reeling that there's been a second death. They don't seem close to an arrest to me. Did you have an alibi for Jo's death?"

He shook his head. "I mean, Anna knows I was home, but I'm not sure she's in the mood to be giving me alibis. I'd had a really exhausting day at a construction site and slept like the dead that night. Even overslept the next morning. Anna knows I was home, though. She really needs to talk to Red. I deserve *that* from her, at least."

Pasha, who'd been looking at Flint with interest, came over to him, holding her tail up in a relaxed manner. Then she proceeded to rub against him as he leaned over to rub her.

"Do you have cats of your own?" asked Myrtle.

He nodded. "Two of them, actually. They've been keeping me company. Anna's there, but *not* there, if you know what I mean. She's been acting really remote lately. I'm getting the feeling that she's not all that interested in saving our marriage. Like I said last time, she's been talking about us getting separated." He gave a short laugh. "Sorry, Miss Myrtle. You're pretty easy to talk to. Maybe you should become a therapist."

Myrtle shrugged. "Old people are easy to talk to because we're difficult to shock. We've heard it all before. But I'm sorry to hear about you and Anna."

Flint gave a gusty sigh. "It was going to be tough no matter what. There's been a lot of trust lost on my end. We used to have good times together . . . lots of nights where we'd just stay in and listen to music or play board games together. Or we'd work around the house like we were a team—I'd be making repairs and she'd be cleaning. But those days are all in the past now." He sounded wistful.

"See if things will still work out. Maybe she's simply got a lot on her mind lately. But don't waste too much time if it seems irredeemable. There's no point beating a dead horse. There are plenty more fish in the sea." She smiled. "If I think of any other aphorisms, I'll be sure to throw them your way."

He smiled back at her. "Thanks. And you're right. I've been so stressed out about our relationship and wondering what's going to happen. I haven't been sleeping, and I've lost weight. But I'm coming around to the point where I'm like . . . I don't have any control over this situation, you know? I can't make Anna do anything. I can't even *influence* her one way or another. So whatever is going to happen is just going to happen. And weirdly, that's sort of comforting to me."

"Qué será, será," said Myrtle, nodding.

Flint looked confused, but nodded, too.

"Do you have any new insight over who might be responsible for these deaths? Last time I spoke with you, you were thinking it might be Victor's brother, Dallas."

Flint sighed. "Yeah. I mean, I like Dallas and all, so I feel bad saying that. But I can't think who else had such a big motive." He stopped and chuckled. "Except for me, I guess. Since I know that *I* didn't do it, I'm thinking it's got to be Dallas. Now that Jo and Victor are gone, Dallas is going to inherit Victor's estate."

Myrtle said, "Actually, I heard from a fairly reliable source that Jo's will indicates her family will inherit Victor's estate. Dallas isn't going to profit off of these crimes." The fairly reliable source was, of course, Dallas himself.

"Whoa. That must have been a punch to Dallas's gut. He probably thought he'd finally have his head above water, and he's getting *nothing*?" He shook his head. Then he was quiet for a few moments. "Maybe Dallas *thought* he'd get the money, though. The fact he was wrong doesn't mean he didn't kill Victor and Jo. It means that it just didn't work out the way he thought it would. I hope Red and them are considering that. Otherwise, it makes me look like suspect number one again."

Myrtle prodded him. "You think so?"

"Sure. I'm the easiest solution, aren't I? Sorry. I just feel like Red doesn't have a lot of imagination."

"Oh, we're in full agreement on that point," assured Myrtle.

"Right. And let's face it; I was upset about Anna. I thought Victor had lured her away. I didn't want to face the fact that Anna might have instigated the whole affair. That she was at fault. That *I* was at fault for not keeping her happy. Besides, Victor was an easy target. He had plenty of money and a wife who loved him and he went after *my* wife? I don't have anything. It made me really resentful, Miss Myrtle, I'm not going to lie."

Myrtle nodded. "Of course it did. It's only natural to feel that way."

"But what makes me mad is that people might think I killed Jo. Why on earth would I do something like that?"

Flint seemed to ask the question genuinely, so Myrtle answered. "I'm not sure people do think that. Maybe the police do. They could be thinking Jo had seen something, and the killer wanted her eliminated."

Flint's brow creased. "But I thought Jo was on the scene after Victor's body was found."

"I suppose Jo could have been by earlier and then come back. Or perhaps she observed something later, and the killer decided to get rid of her, too."

Flint shook his head. "It's all a mess. Such a mess. I hope Red finds out who did this, and fast. I'm not going to be able to sleep until he does."

"Yes, I'm pulling for him too," said Myrtle, crossing her fingers behind her back as she fibbed. She was certainly not pulling for Red. In fact, she was fairly certain she herself was going to be completely responsible for ensuring the killer was safely behind bars.

Flint looked at his watch and made a face. "Well, I guess I've been chatting your ear off for long enough. Sorry about that. I better get onto that fence."

"Do you need me to show you the panels that need fixing?"

Flint said, "No, ma'am. I saw them from the roof when I was cleaning out your gutters last time. No worries; I'll take care of the fence."

"Thank you. And watch out for Erma Sherman. She's incurably nosy and is sure to come running out and bore you to death with all her medical ailments."

He grinned at her. "Thanks for the tip."

It took Flint only an hour or so to mend the fence. Then he cheerfully went on his way, check in hand. Myrtle took a look at her bank account online. As she suspected, the balance was exceedingly low. Perhaps she shouldn't have had Flint come over twice in the same social security pay period. But how else was she going to speak with him? She could hardly have scouted out various construction sites around town trying to find him.

She was going to be needing very cheap entertainment until her next check came. For Myrtle, this meant a trip to the local library. Besides, she had a book that was due the following day, and she didn't think paying a fine, no matter how small, would help her financial situation.

Myrtle tossed her book in her tremendous purse and, cane in hand, headed off to the library. It was a pleasant day and a nice walk. The street downtown was lined with trees blowing gently in the wind. Kids were biking, the birds were singing. It was idyllic. But even in that perfect setting, Myrtle's mind drifted back to murder.

Her reverie was broken by the sound of her phone ringing from somewhere deep inside her purse. Myrtle muttered to herself as she rummaged through papers, tissue containers, and loose change as the phone continued merrily ringing. She finally grabbed it. "Hello?" she demanded.

"It's me."

Myrtle said, "Miles? I thought you'd still be recuperating from the funeral."

"Oh, I am. I had a nap, actually. But Georgia called me up."

Myrtle snorted. "That must have thrown you. You always have this very odd reaction to Georgia. Why did she call?"

Miles sighed. "She wanted me to help her lug out her belongings into the yard again tomorrow evening. Georgia decided that having her previous yard sale cut short by murder meant that her objective hadn't been reached. She still needed more stuff sold." He paused. "So she could buy more stuff. It's an approach that I don't find very logical."

"That's because it isn't. Georgia simply enjoys acquiring new things. When she ran out of space for the new things, she sold some so that she could continue the process. I'm assuming that you made an excuse not to help her?"

Miles waffled. "I told her I'd think about it."

"What is there to think about?" demanded Myrtle. "You don't want to spend your time pulling angels out into Georgia's front yard. Case closed."

Miles said, "She just seemed so excited about having another yard sale. I didn't want to disappoint her."

"We really need to work on your 'saying no' skills, Miles. I thought you'd gotten better at that."

Miles said, "I have. I can definitely say no one-hundred percent of the time when it comes to an email request. With the phone, it's probably 50-50." He paused. "The thing that worried me the most about her request was it sounded like it was going to be a real pain. Georgia said she was going to be much more organized with the process this time. She was talking about spreadsheets and placing things where she can keep an eye on them. Georgia said people had stolen her merchandise last time."

"Georgia thought someone had stolen her stuff? All those tchotchkes? I think she has an inflated opinion of the worth of the things she put out there. Besides, Georgia should be more concerned about more dead bodies at her yard sale. She probably sold one of the items and forgot she had." Then something occurred to Myrtle. "Wait. Was one of the missing items an angel?"

"Good guess," said Miles dryly. "It's not as if she doesn't have scads of them."

"Mmm," said Myrtle in a vague voice. There was something there. Something had popped into her head. "I've got to go."

"But what should I do?" asked Miles.

"Hmm? Oh. Tell Georgia that you've pulled something. We're not young people, Miles. It happens. Bye."

She stopped short in the street so she could put her phone away, this time into a place where she could more easily retrieve it. As she did, someone cursed behind her.

Myrtle turned. "Gracious. That's a real mess."

Millicent Montgomery was covered with a chocolate milkshake. She glowered at Myrtle. "It wouldn't have happened if you hadn't stopped like that."

"It wouldn't have happened if you hadn't been holding a milkshake without a lid," said Myrtle tartly.

Millicent opened her mouth to retort, saw Myrtle's face and thought better of it, and slunk away.

Myrtle continued to the library, her thoughts still on her conversation with Miles. She considered getting on the computer there, but decided it could wait until she got into the privacy of her own home. Instead, she returned the library book, found an intriguing science fiction novel (she did try to read broadly), and then checked out several music CDs so she could hear something new at home.

The librarian smiled at her, "Found some good music? You know I keep telling you that you can check out music online and listen to it on your phone."

Myrtle gave her a good-natured scowl. "I know, I know. But while you still have physical copies of the music, I'll keep doing what I'm doing. There's something satisfying about snapping a CD into a player. I feel the same about DVDs. It's not that I'm a luddite, you know."

The librarian frowned at her. "Luddite?"

"Someone who resists the lure of technology," said Myrtle.

The librarian said swiftly, "It's because you *aren't* a luddite that I keep suggesting it. If you're happy with the physical copies, then keep checking them out. The nice thing is that I get to keep seeing your smiling face."

This made Myrtle laugh, as the librarian intended. "There's your smile," she said. "You looked like you had something very serious on your mind."

"I do," admitted Myrtle. "But having a break from thinking about it is very nice."

Once she was back home, she popped in one of the CDs and sat on her sofa. It was time for her to figure things out. She thought she had all the pieces. Myrtle pulled out her phone to look something up. When it suddenly started ringing, she jumped.

"Elaine!" said Myrtle. "How are you today? And, perhaps even more importantly, how is Jack?"

"We're both doing really well. I see you've had Flint over again, doing some work."

Myrtle said, "Indeed I have. It would definitely have been cheaper to have Red do it, but he's so tied up with the investigation that I know he wouldn't have been able to get to it for ages."

Elaine gave a wry chuckle. "For sure. Plus, we have a ton of halfway finished projects over at our house. Red always seems to have something come up when it's time to work on them."

Myrtle felt more cheerful about her account then. "Then it's good I had Flint come take care of it."

Elaine said, "I was wondering if you wanted to go to the duck pond with Jack and me to feed the ducks. I figure you could probably use a break from the case."

Elaine knew her mother-in-law well. Not only was Myrtle working hard on figuring out the same case Red was working on, but she needed a bit of a break. Not necessarily from the case itself, but from thinking about it. It was fairly making her head spin, considering all the different possibilities. Perhaps a short break would help her make sense of it all.

"That sounds perfect," said Myrtle.

"I can come pick you up," said Elaine quickly.

Myrtle walked over to glance out her front window. Elaine's minivan wasn't there in the driveway. "No need to bother! I can meet you there."

"It's quite a walk," said Elaine. "I can be there in just a few minutes."

"No, the walk will do me good. I need to have my head cleared out a little. I've barely had time to think with all the goings-on. Do you need me to bring some food for the ducks?"

Elaine said, "No, we're all good. I've got birdseed I'm going to feed them."

"Heavens! That's fancy. Red and I used to just feed them stale bread when he was a boy. They loved it."

Elaine refrained from saying that bread was about the worst thing you can feed ducks. She said, "Oh, the birdseed was pretty cheap, and I've got plenty of it. Maybe there'll even be some interesting birds there. I'll bring my camera too, and my field book. Oh, and I have this wonderful app on my phone. It helps me recognize birds by sight *and* by song."

Myrtle suspected that having a brilliant, but noisy, preschooler would ensure the birds might not want to stick around. "Sounds good, Elaine. What time were you thinking?"

"I've still got a couple of errands to run. How about if we meet there in thirty minutes?"

"Perfect," said Myrtle. But instead of waiting, she grabbed her cane and headed to the door. The whole point of the exercise, besides seeing Elaine and her wonderful grandson, was to give her brain some space to think. Sitting around her house was decidedly not helping.

Before shutting the door behind her, she looked back into the house at Pasha, who was blinking sleepily at her. "Want to stay in, my darling girl? Or do you fancy a walk?"

Pasha hesitated. The sofa was very comfortable, and there was a lovely sunbeam that was crossing over it right where her tummy was. But the wide, wonderful world beckoned, and she quickly hopped up and padded over to Myrtle.

"Let's go," said Myrtle cheerfully.

Pasha was a most remarkable cat. She walked beside Myrtle as they headed in the direction of the duck pond. It was a beautiful Thursday—not too hot and not too cold. People waved at her from their cars as they passed by.

Once they got to the duck pond, Myrtle was pleased to see there was an open bench. Not only was there a single open bench, there were many of them. In fact, the duck pond was blissfully quiet. Weeping willows stood gracefully on the banks of the pond. There were mallards in the water, which made Myrtle even more pleased. Elaine would like the pretty mallards. They'd make for better pictures than the white ducks that were so often there.

Pasha jumped up on the bench with her. She was very alert and somewhat edgy.

"Lots of birds for you to look at," murmured Myrtle. "But don't annihilate any of them. Elaine would be so disappointed."

Pasha kept glancing around, her head turning in various directions. Her pupils were large.

Myrtle leaned back on the bench, setting her cane beside her. She absently rubbed Pasha in the hopes of helping her settle down. As she did, she started thinking about the murders. Something continued to bother her. She thought about it. The most significant recent discovery seemed to be that Kingston was present at the yard sale. Not only that, but that Kingston spotted *Dallas* at the yard sale. Those were two people who'd originally claimed they hadn't been there. With their alibis in tatters, surely they should be the ones Myrtle needed to investigate further.

But somehow, she didn't think that was it. Kingston and Dallas hadn't been bothering her. Millicent, however, was. She often tried *not* to think about Millicent because the woman tended to get on her nerves. But there was something about her that was bugging her even more than usual.

Pasha started to get even more jittery than she already was. A crow flew overhead, cawing at them. Pasha practically leaped from her skin.

"It's all right, sweetness," crooned Myrtle. "Those crows wouldn't be fun for you to take on. They're very smart. Probably as smart as you are. And they're huge."

Myrtle started thinking about everything she knew about Millicent. The woman had a tremendous chip on her shoulder, for one. She felt wronged by Victor profiting from her property. Millicent seemed very motivated in terms of her resale business and had invested what seemed to be a lot of time and energy in getting things set up. She'd been shadowing Victor during his yard sale jaunts. How had Victor felt about that? Myrtle couldn't imagine Victor would have been pleased. Would he have taunted her? Told her to back off?

Pasha growled, looking around her.

"It's okay, sweetheart," said Myrtle vaguely. "That old crow isn't going to bother you."

Myrtle took out her phone because she felt she still hadn't put her finger on what the issue was with Millicent. Besides her own dislike for the woman, of course. She Googled her and saw the article in the *Bradley Bugle* about Victor was the very first entry. Considering the fact that the wire had picked up on the story and other newspapers had carried it meant that there were a lot of hits. The article was the one the paper had done with Victor in which he said he'd resold the first edition James Bond book for a mint of money. The way Victor had talked about Millicent in the story made her look careless, foolish, or possibly both. Millicent likely hated the fact Google listed that story first on any search result of her.

Myrtle looked at the next entry, which was Millicent's online storefront. Myrtle wasn't completely sure she could tell how good Millicent's offerings were, but she looked closely at the page. There were vinyl records that didn't seem to be in the best of condition. There were dolls, which looked sweet, but hardly collectors' items. Then she stared at one item and clicked on it.

It was one of Georgia's angels. This, in itself, seemed to indicate that perhaps Millicent wasn't good at gauging the worth of items. But then Myrtle looked more closely at it. She recognized this one. It had been lying near Victor when she'd discovered him, dead. And here it was on Millicent's website, for sale.

Which was precisely when she heard a cold voice behind her. "I had a feeling I needed to keep an eye on you."

Chapter Eighteen

Myrtle spun around. Pasha spat angrily, fur standing on end. Millicent stood there, glowering at her.

"You're just as nosy as I thought. And a lot smarter than I thought, too."

Myrtle couldn't help preening just a little at her smartness. "Yes. Well, unfortunately, you weren't as clever as you should have been through this whole thing. How did you think you could get away with this? Hubris?"

Millicent frowned. "Hubris? You believe I think pretty highly of myself, don't you?"

"Killers often do." Myrtle slowly wrapped her hand around her cane. "There's one thing I'm curious about, though. Why did you have to kill Jo? What did she see?"

Millicent's eyes were expressionless as she stepped closer. "She was acting stupid. It was her fault."

Myrtle raised her eyebrows. "Really? You're seriously going to blame the victim?"

"Of course. She deserved it."

Myrtle said, "Wait, let me guess. Jo was actually at the yard sale twice, wasn't she? Before Victor died and then after."

"Well, if you know the story, you should tell it yourself." Her voice was cold.

Myrtle, feeling rather pleased with herself, despite the circumstances, continued. "Jo wanted to get back together with Victor, despite having an affair. Maybe the affair simply solidified things for her. Jo realized Victor, flaws and all, was the man for her."

Millicent rolled her eyes. "Whatever."

Myrtle ignored the interjection. "I'm guessing Jo wanted to find a chance to speak with Victor and tell him how she felt. But he hadn't been taking her phone calls. She'd have known that he'd be at Georgia's yard sale. He was at *every* yard sale. Plus, Georgia was locally renowned for her collections of novelty items. So Jo showed up."

Millicent said, "Well, you got that right. She was there for a while and then left."

"She most likely left because she wasn't going to have a moment to get Victor by himself. You were following him around. Tailing him."

Millicent sniffed. "Learning from him."

Now it was Myrtle's turn to roll her eyes. "Well, your learning was not done in a way that gave Victor much personal space. And I'm going to guess again. I think Victor took the opportunity to jeer at you or taunt you. You said he was like that. So Jo also probably saw you both squabbling." Her hand tightened on her cane again.

Millicent was quiet at this.

Myrtle continued, "Jo left, realizing she may not have the chance to talk privately to Victor. When she got back home, maybe she gave herself a pep-talk. At any rate, she squared her shoulders and headed back over to Georgia's house to see if Victor was still there. When she found out Victor was dead, you were the first person she blamed."

"Because she knew Victor and I had words over my James Bond book," said Millicent in a defensive tone.

"Maybe. But the more she thought about it, the more stock she put into you tailing him at the yard sale. It had seemed insignificant before, but it was more ominous knowing Victor was dead."

Millicent tired of it. "All right, you figured it out. She saw Victor and me fussing with each other and him ducking behind the hanging rug to get away. I guess the more she thought about it, the more she wanted to know if our fussing had gotten out of control. If you're such a smarty-pants, why are you giving me ammunition against you? You know what I am."

Pasha, not liking Millicent's tone, was making a low growling sound to warn her off.

"Get rid of that cat before I do," snarled Millicent.

Which was exactly when Myrtle decided to get rid of Millicent, instead. She swung the cane as hard as she could from her seated position. She heard a satisfying crack and a yelp from Millicent. However, her awkward position meant Millicent could grab the cane from her.

Pasha, sensing the danger, bounded a few yards away before proceeding to spit and hiss at Millicent. Then she yowled as loud as she could, sounding like several angry cats instead of just one.

Millicent grabbed Myrtle's cell phone and tossed it into the duck pond. The mallards scattered quickly.

Myrtle scrambled to buy time. She needed to grab the cane back from Millicent, disable her, and then get away. She certainly didn't want Elaine and little Jack to come up on this scene.

Who knew what Millicent might be capable of? As far as Myrtle knew, the annoying Millicent could potentially be packing heat in that silly-looking purse of hers.

Pasha, apparently fearing Myrtle was not only endangered but also potentially incompetent, launched herself at Millicent.

Millicent shrieked. "Get your cat off of me!"

Myrtle, who had no intention of doing so, grabbed for her cane. But Millicent was too quick and pulled back on it.

Which was when an earsplitting horn began booming from behind them.

Millicent, startled, eased her grip on the cane, and Myrtle was finally successful in retrieving it. The ungodly honking continued. Not only that, but Myrtle could tell that Elaine, with her free, non-honking hand, was filming Myrtle's struggle with Millicent on her phone.

Millicent apparently saw the same thing because she dashed away. Although Myrtle wasn't at all sure where she was heading, since her car was near Elaine, and Millicent was running in the opposite direction. Myrtle hurried to the minivan.

"I'd never have thought a minivan's horn could sound like that," said Myrtle, gasping a little from her trot to the car.

"It's pretty ferocious," said Elaine grimly. "Myrtle, are you all right?"

"Yes, but we need to follow her. She's going to get away."

Elaine shook her head. "We don't have to worry. Before I started honking, I got Red on the phone. He's coming over with the state police, and he sounded as mad as a wet hen."

"Well, at least this time I didn't do anything to make him irritated. You tell him I was simply here to feed the ducks with my grandson."

Elaine said, "And solve the case! Don't forget that. It's not exactly insignificant. That's a *big deal*."

"Yaaayyy!" agreed Jack from the backseat as Myrtle and Elaine laughed.

"Okay," said Elaine, starting up the car. "With that being said, we're going to get out of here."

"Yes," said Myrtle. "Lurking in a spot where a known murderer was just seen would be a recipe for disaster."

Elaine kindly refrained from stating that Myrtle, if anyone, should definitely know about recipes and disaster colliding.

"Back to my house, then? For a little birdwatching?" asked Myrtle.

"Ducks!" said Jack, suddenly realizing his mother wasn't moving them in the correct direction for feeding mallards.

"You know, I have the feeling you might be a bit of a target right now, Myrtle. Let's go to my house. I don't think Millicent would be quite brave enough to storm the police chief's house. I'll text Red to let him know."

A few minutes later, they were back at Elaine's. Jack was bereft that ducks weren't being fed, so they entertained him by turning on his favorite show. Ordinarily, Myrtle would have played trucks with Jack instead, but her mind was whirling too much to manage it right then.

Elaine seemed to realize that. "He's all settled and happy. Let's fix you a little drink."

"Oh, I'm probably fine." It was a fairly unconvincing rejection.

"I have sherry," said Elaine.

"Well, maybe just a few sips. It's been quite the day. Will you join me?"

Elaine shook her head. "Not this time. I'm not sure I won't be driving the car later. Of course, if Millicent isn't captured, I suppose I'll be staying in."

Myrtle took a tiny sip of her sherry. "I do wish Red would give us some sort of update." She paused. "Let's talk about other things so the time will pass quicker."

Elaine said, "Oh, I do have a little gossipy something! I know Flint was over doing work at your place earlier. When I was out running errands, I saw him sitting on a bench with Patty from my coffee group."

"Single-mom-Patty?" asked Myrtle with interest.

Elaine nodded. "They were both laughing and seemed to be hitting it off really well."

"Well, I'm glad. He's a nice fellow. And I'm sure he'll be relieved to hear that he's not a murder suspect anymore."

It was a full hour later when they finally heard a key in the front door. Myrtle breathed out a sigh of relief. Red wouldn't be here if Millicent was still on the loose. He'd be out there searching for her and plenty irritated, to boot.

"Daddy!" Jack abandoned the increasingly frenetic, animated TV show he was watching to run over and hug Red's legs.

He reached down and swung the little boy up for a hug before setting him back down again and watching him re-engage with the TV. Red looked tired, but there was a gleam in his eyes that Myrtle recognized.

"You got her," said Myrtle.

"Yep. We sure did. Perkins is on his way over now to debrief you," said Red. He glanced at the sherry bottle. "You doing okay, Mama?"

"Yes. The sherry has calmed my nerves a little. Would you like some? Of your own sherry?" Myrtle smiled.

Red shook his head. "I'm still on duty. Even if I wasn't, beer would be my pick." He joined his mother and Elaine at the kitchen table. "I'm beat. And I think I need to spend some time on the treadmill at the gym."

Elaine gave him a sympathetic look. "Lots of running this afternoon?"

"Lots of running, taking wrong steps, stumbling, crashing through undergrowth, you name it. But we got her."

Myrtle said, "It sounds like she led you on a merry chase."

There was a tap at the door, and Red jumped up to open it. As expected, Perkins was standing there.

"Come on in," said Red. "Excuse the sound of cartoons. It's going to make for a really incongruous background to the story Mama's going to tell us."

Perkins gave Myrtle his polite smile and settled at the table with them. "Would anyone like coffee?" asked Elaine.

Perkins hesitated, clearly not wanting to be the only one who accepted. Red said, "Oh, I'll take most of the pot of coffee, if you make it."

Myrtle didn't usually have regular coffee so late in the day, but had the sneaking suspicion that she wasn't going to be able to sleep that night anyway. "I might as well have a cup, too."

Red muttered something under his breath about caffeine and his mother wandering the streets all night. But he didn't say anything to her about it.

Perkins gave Myrtle a smile. "You've done it again!"

"Nearly gotten herself killed, you mean?" asked Red.

Perkins and Myrtle ignored him. Myrtle beamed at Perkins. "I suppose I have, haven't I?" She attempted to sound modest but failed utterly.

Perkins said, "Could you walk me through what happened?"

Chapter Nineteen

Red muttered something under his breath. Myrtle glared at him. "I don't make assignations with potential killers at remote locations, if that's what you think. Elaine, Jack, and I were going to feed the ducks. It was all very above-board and preschool friendly."

"I can verify that," said Elaine.

"You and Elaine met there, I'm supposing," said Perkins.

"That's right. Elaine was wrapping up errands, and I decided a walk and some fresh air would do me good. I set off to the park with Pasha."

Perkins said, "Oh, you had a friend with you."

"Certainly."

Red said, "It's a feral cat, Perkins."

"Right. I do remember Pasha now. Please continue, Mrs. Clover."

Myrtle said, "Elaine? May I borrow your phone? Mine is at the bottom of the duck pond."

Elaine handed her phone right over. Myrtle picked it up and started typing something in as everyone stared at her.

"Can you play with the phone later, Mama? Perkins and I have work to do," said Red.

Myrtle persisted in perusing Elaine's phone while the others glanced at each other and sipped their coffee. Finally, Myrtle said, "As I suspected. Lladró angels are indeed worth something."

"Pardon?" asked Perkins.

"Georgia's yard sale had all sorts of things in it. Georgia loved collecting angels, but she'd completely run out of room. It seems Georgia might enjoy the *collecting* aspect almost more than the possession of the things. She needed to clear some space so that she could continue her collecting."

Perkins said, "And one of the angels was valuable?"

"Yes. Or *fairly* valuable. The intrinsic value of the item wasn't something that was important to Georgia. She's not into reselling like Millicent and Victor were. So she just put a few angels out for sale. One of the porcelain figurines was an angel with a mandolin. From what I see online, it's worth about $750." She slid the phone back across the table to Elaine.

Elaine said, "How does that connect with Millicent?"

Myrtle said, "When Miles and I came across Victor's body, he'd dropped a handful of items that he'd plucked up from Georgia's sale. In the shock of discovering Victor dead, I'd ignored the items. Until I saw the angel for sale in Millicent's online store."

Red frowned. "So you saw the angel. Then Millicent swooped in and took the angel? Wouldn't you have noticed that right away?"

"There was a tremendous distraction. A woman was shrieking bloody murder when she saw Victor. Everyone came rushing over, including Millicent. Remember, a yard sale was still in progress at that point. Victor's body had been concealed behind some hanging items. As well, there were still a couple of things lying near Victor. Bigger items than the angel."

Perkins said slowly, "I'm trying to follow, but there are some spots I'm unsure about. Wouldn't Millicent have taken the angel and other items right after killing Victor? Why did she have to return later? And why take the angel and nothing else?"

Myrtle beamed at him. She loved the opportunity to show off more than anything else in the world. And Perkins had given her that chance. "Millicent killed Victor out of anger for his realizing the value of an old book of hers and then exploiting its value. At the time, it wasn't connected to the items he'd gotten at Georgia's sale."

Red rubbed his face. "Why on earth would Millicent Montgomery decide to take out Victor in such a public place? And it wasn't like it was just yesterday that he'd resold that book of hers—it's been a while. Had she lost her mind?"

"Victor had been taunting her. Smirking. But then, Millicent had been annoying him by following him around yard sales and swooping down on anything he paid attention to. She couldn't even trust that he wasn't spoofing her, either. That must have been frustrating for her."

"Spoofing her?" asked Perkins.

"Victor was apparently studiously considering some worthless junk just so Millicent could think it valuable and buy it before he had the opportunity. She'd realize later when she looked the item up online that it was completely worthless. But it must have been very annoying to Victor to have Millicent trailing him around."

Perkins said, "So we're thinking Victor was likely mocking Millicent or taunting her somehow. She loses her temper and strikes him with whatever was at hand."

Myrtle nodded. "She was probably shocked at what happened. And afraid someone would come upon them and realize what she'd done. She left the scene. But maybe she was still thinking about the items that Victor had dropped. She couldn't be *sure* they were valuable, but they *could* have been. And wouldn't it have been almost as if she were getting back at Victor? So when the distraction happened, she swiped the angel."

"But nothing else." Red frowned.

Myrtle shrugged. "Maybe she thought if she took everything around him, someone would notice there were no items lying near Victor anymore. But if she just took one, it could be overlooked. Plus, it was the smallest of the items. And it worked, for the most part. For a while, I didn't remember there was something missing."

"Until you did," said Perkins with a smile.

Myrtle beamed again at him. "Miles helped."

Before she could explain how very helpful Miles had been in the resolution of the case, Red jumped in. "Okay, I got what happened with Victor. Millicent flipped out on him after a build-up of bad feelings. Why Jo Fowler?"

Myrtle said, "Jo actually blamed Millicent right away for killing Victor. You were there, remember?"

Red looked grim. "Yeah. But I figured it was just Jo lashing out because she was upset. Because she knew Millicent and Victor had had words."

"Well, it ended up being more than that. Jo showed up earlier at the yard sale. We know from Kingston that Jo still held a torch for Victor, despite her affair. Maybe she wanted to catch up with Victor but couldn't bring herself to talk to him, especially with Millicent following him around. The stakes were pretty high; Jo wanted to repair their marriage. He hadn't been taking her calls. She could have freaked herself out, left the yard sale and gone back home to give herself a pep talk. When she returned to the yard sale, Victor was already dead."

Perkins knit his brows. "So you're thinking Jo saw something the first time she was at the yard sale."

"Right. Millicent said Victor and she were squabbling, and Jo had seen her shove Victor so they were both behind the hanging rug. Jo approached Millicent about it. It made Millicent decide to get rid of Jo once and for all."

Perkins said, "Fortunately, we have forensic evidence from Jo Fowler's crime scene. Once we search Millicent's house and collect DNA evidence, I don't think we'll have a problem making a connection."

The doorbell rang. Red muttered something under his breath about his house being a circus. It was actually a very pertinent remark because Jack's TV show was just featuring a circus and a pair of frenetic, animated acrobats.

"Miles! Come on in," said Red. "Mama's here."

"She's all right then?" asked Miles. "I saw the police cars here and when your mother didn't open the door, I was worried."

"Fine and dandy and drinking a sherry. Would you like one?" asked Red.

"Maybe just a small one."

Red quickly moved an extra chair around the kitchen table, and Miles took a seat. He took a small sip of the sherry Red handed to him.

"Is it all over?" Miles asked anxiously.

Perkins greeted him and then said, "Millicent Montgomery is under arrest. We're searching her home now and hope to find the clothing she wore to the yard sale. We believe it may match fibers found on the victim's body."

Miles glanced over at Myrtle, as if suspecting he might be missing out on a very interesting part of the story.

Myrtle smirked at him. "Millicent tried to do away with me. But she didn't get far."

"Clearly," said Miles. He sounded relieved.

Myrtle said, "She and I struggled, and she didn't immediately win. Then Elaine showed up and scared her off." She paused. "Pasha was quite courageous, as well. I had lots of help this time."

"You were saying Miles was one of the folks who helped you figure things out," prompted Red.

Myrtle said, "Yes. Georgia asked Miles to help her move her yard sale stuff back outside tomorrow evening."

Miles blushed. "I would have helped Georgia. It's just that my family was in town, and I'm in need of a rest."

Myrtle waved her hand dismissively. "That doesn't really matter. The point is that you told me she'd called you. And that it sounded like it wasn't just a matter of lugging things back inside. She was also trying to keep an inventory of her things. You thought it would be more trouble than you were up for."

Perkins asked, "And something about the inventory was off?"

Miles suddenly realized the direction Myrtle's mind was heading in. "Yes. She mentioned she thought people were stealing from her at the yard sale. Which, sadly, I didn't take very seriously. It seemed like Georgia might have an inflated notion of the value of her items."

"Do you remember what, in particular, Georgia mentioned was missing?"

Miles nodded. "One of her angels."

Myrtle gave a satisfied smile.

Red was still frowning thunderously. "So how did Millicent Montgomery realize that you knew about the missing angel? Did she know you were making a connection? Or was she trying to figure out if you'd put it all together or not?"

Myrtle said, "Well, I was hoping she hadn't overheard a phone conversation I'd had, but she clearly did. I was catching up with Miles, and he was telling me about the fact Georgia needed help giving the yard sale again. He mentioned the missing item, and I asked him if it was an angel."

Miles nodded, remembering. "You said that right away."

"That's when I recalled that there had been an angel lying next to Victor. It was fairly theatrical-looking at the time, but not nearly as theatrical as his dead body."

Perkins said, "You were out in public when Miles called?"

"I was downtown. On my way to the library, actually. And I saw Millicent not long after. Actually, she ran right into me and covered herself with a milkshake. That must have been when she overheard me and realized I was onto her."

Perkins asked, "But *were* you onto her then? Or were you still putting the pieces together? Because there was nothing that Mr. Bradford said that suggested one particular person."

"True. But Millicent didn't do herself any favors by showing up right at that second. It made me start thinking of her. Plus, she was acting rather awkward when I saw her. At the time, I thought she might be behaving that way because she had spilled something all over herself. But now it's clear she was worried about me. Anyway, I continued over to the library, ran that errand, and then headed home. Elaine and I made plans, then I walked over here. I looked up Millicent's online store on my phone and spotted an angel for sale. It looked just like the one I'd seen lying next to Victor. And the rest is history." Myrtle shrugged.

Red said grimly, "The rest is caught on video, you mean. Mama, she was very close to murdering you, too."

"We were just going to feed the ducks," said Elaine loyally. Myrtle smiled at her with appreciation. It was good that Elaine actually had a useful hobby for once. If she hadn't been so interested in birdwatching, Myrtle might not have made it out of the park alive.

Perkins said, "Well, you did an amazing job, Mrs. Clover. We've put a dangerous person behind bars, and it's all thanks to you."

Myrtle gloated.

"A round of applause for Myrtle!" said Elaine. And everyone joined in, even Red.

"Yayyyyy!" said Jack, abandoning his cartoon to join them. He hugged Myrtle's leg.

Red stood up. "I guess Perkins and I should head over to the station to have a chat with Millicent. It should be an interesting one. What're you doing the rest of the day, Mama? I certainly hope it's going to involve staying at home."

"Well, eventually it's going to involve writing an article for Sloan. But, in the meantime, I do believe I'm going to sit in front of my television. How about you, Miles? Are you up for that?"

Miles, relieved that she didn't mention their soap opera by name this time, said, "That sounds like the perfect afternoon."

And, surrounded by crossword puzzles, a bit more sherry, and a snoring black cat, it was.

About the Author

Elizabeth writes the Southern Quilting mysteries and Memphis Barbeque mysteries for Penguin Random House and the Myrtle Clover series for Midnight Ink and independently. She blogs at ElizabethSpannCraig.com/blog, named by Writer's Digest as one of the 101 Best Websites for Writers. Elizabeth makes her home in Matthews, North Carolina, with her husband. She's the mother of two.

Sign up for Elizabeth's free newsletter to stay updated on releases:

https://bit.ly/2xZUXqO

This and That

I love hearing from my readers. You can find me on Facebook as Elizabeth Spann Craig Author, on Twitter as elizabethscraig, on my website at elizabethspanncraig.com, and by email at elizabethspanncraig@gmail.com.

Thanks so much for reading my book...I appreciate it. If you enjoyed the story, would you please leave a short review on the site where you purchased it? Just a few words would be great. Not only do I feel encouraged reading them, but they also help other readers discover my books. Thank you!

Did you know my books are available in print and ebook formats? Most of the Myrtle Clover series is available in audio and some of the Southern Quilting mysteries are. Find the audiobooks here: https://elizabethspanncraig.com/audio/

Please follow me on BookBub for my reading recommendations and release notifications.

I'd also like to thank some folks who helped me put this book together. Thanks to my cover designer, Karri Klawiter, for her awesome covers. Thanks to my editor, Judy Beatty for her help. Thanks to beta readers Amanda Arrieta, Rebecca Wahr, Cassie Kelley, and Dan Harris for all of their helpful suggestions and careful reading. Thanks to my ARC readers for helping to spread the word. Thanks, as always, to my family and readers.

Other Works by Elizabeth

Myrtle Clover Series in Order (be sure to look for the Myrtle series in audio, ebook, and print):

Pretty is as Pretty Dies

Progressive Dinner Deadly

A Dyeing Shame

A Body in the Backyard

Death at a Drop-In

A Body at Book Club

Death Pays a Visit

A Body at Bunco

Murder on Opening Night

Cruising for Murder

Cooking is Murder

A Body in the Trunk

Cleaning is Murder

Edit to Death

Hushed Up

A Body in the Attic

Murder on the Ballot

Death of a Suitor

A Dash of Murder

Death at a Diner

A Myrtle Clover Christmas

Murder at a Yard Sale

Doom and Bloom (late 2023)

Southern Quilting Mysteries in Order:

Quilt or Innocence
Knot What it Seams
Quilt Trip
Shear Trouble
Tying the Knot
Patch of Trouble
Fall to Pieces
Rest in Pieces
On Pins and Needles
Fit to be Tied
Embroidering the Truth
Knot a Clue
Quilt-Ridden
Needled to Death
A Notion to Murder
Crosspatch
Behind the Seams
Quilt Complex (2023)

The Village Library Mysteries in Order (Debuting 2019):

Checked Out
Overdue
Borrowed Time
Hush-Hush
Where There's a Will
Frictional Characters
Spine Tingling
A Novel Idea
End of Story

Memphis Barbeque Mysteries in Order (Written as Riley Adams):

Delicious and Suspicious

Finger Lickin' Dead

Hickory Smoked Homicide

Rubbed Out

And a standalone "cozy zombie" novel: Race to Refuge, written as Liz Craig

Made in United States
North Haven, CT
18 June 2023

37939128R00124